THE EMANCIPATION OF FELA MOORE

LANO AKIWUMI

Bloomington, IN 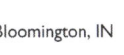  Milton Keynes, UK

authorHOUSE®

AuthorHouse™
1663 Liberty Drive, Suite 200
Bloomington, IN 47403
www.authorhouse.com
Phone: 1-800-839-8640

AuthorHouse™ UK Ltd.
500 Avebury Boulevard
Central Milton Keynes, MK9 2BE
www.authorhouse.co.uk
Phone: 08001974150

This book is a work of fiction. People, places, events, and situations are the product of the author's imagination. Any resemblance to actual persons, living or dead, or historical events, is purely coincidental.

First published by AuthorHouse   10/23/2006

ISBN: 1-4259-6207-6 (sc)

Printed in the United States of America
Bloomington, Indiana

This book is printed on acid-free paper.

About The Author

LANO AKIWUMI is a writer, lyricist, mentor and youth leader who is dedicated to making a positive difference in his community. Born and raised in North London, he is no stranger to the daily challenges of urban living. His passion is to see young people make the right decisions and avoid many of the mistakes he made growing up. Lano holds a degree in Social Science with Creative and media writing, and he is currently a resident of Haringey, North London where he serves as a youth Minister.

Dedications

This book is dedicated to all the people who know what it means to struggle and overcome.

I would like firstly to thank my Lord and Saviour Jesus Christ the greatest of all overcomers! You are my Alpha and Omega, my Beginning and my End, and I want to thank you for the inspiration to write this book. I believe whoever You've purposed to read it will and I'm at peace with that.

I would like to send a shout out to those who helped proof read my book: Cousin Temi, Cousin Ibi, Emu, Tasha and Tracey. I value all your input and I'm blessed by the fact that you took time out to support a brother. Much love. Thank you.

I also gotta holla at my family and my friends for all the love you've shown me over the years. You know I'm repping for you guys. Thanks for the love.

Peace

Introduction

In every culture and social system, people are having to constantly redefine who they are in a world that is fast-changing. In order that they may fit in, many choose to engage in subcultures, social movements, gangs and antisocial behaviour.

The idea of belonging has been around since the beginning of human existence in the form of the family and also community. However in a time where people are becoming more self-centred instead of being "their brothers keeper ", some members of society get left out and are marginalised.

Jesus said "Thou shalt love thy neighbour as thyself." [1] Whether one believes in Jesus or not, the benefits of His teaching are evident for all to see. The reason why there are so many young people turning to crime and gangs is because they are looking for a place where they will find loyalty and protection in what can often be a hostile environment. In a world where it feels like no-one cares about you, many people are hardened and become defensive.

The race to get rich and be the best serves as a mechanism to keep people from building authentic

---

[1] see the Bible (Mathew 22:39)

relationships and looking out for others. We are so busy that we don't have time to visit family or friends and even sometimes to talk on the phone. Obviously we have to work, however we should never allow a desire to have more commodities, be the thing that drives us to work harder.

Many people are caught in the never ending cycle of trying to "keep up with the Jones' " . This only keeps people as slaves to the latest trends and fashions. Whilst following everyone else they get *lost* in the crowd and are unable to *find* who they really are. Question: Are you pulling the strings or are the strings pulling you?

The Emancipation of Fela Moore is intended to be a vehicle by which you are taken into the world of someone who is on a journey to free himself from the chains that hold many bound. It is a story about liberation, identity, purpose, faith, love and unity—concepts we are all familiar with. *The Emancipation of Fela Moore* was not written as an answer to all the problems in the world but is given as a gift to inspire thought and to challenge people to seek truth because "The truth shall make you free." [2]

---

[2] see the Bible (John 8:32)

Ascension Poem

My Ascension
It stems from my sense of purpose
I'm like a bird in flight that's just learnt it
Christ reclaimed my soul from the teeth of the serpent
No longer a fallen person
To Eden returning
Wid da mental bliss of a temple fixed
We gotta have heaven in ourselves
Before ever having a heaven in this world
The physical realm
Is a manifestation of the spiritual realm
My bredrins a thug, he said that his world's bitter
I told him "this world is like a self-mirror
It reflects the soul in a clear picture"
You reap what you sow
That's the scripture
I grip the, Microphone
And spin the, wheel of fortune to the right cuz yo
I'm clock-wise, not like them guys
Who are anti-clock-wise, trapped in a lost mind
I sit and philosophise wid the top guys on da streets
You don't need a PhD to stay free
Me I just simply pray on my knees
The words of Christ edify my soul
Beyond the level any mind could know
Many say "God? No don't go
That's the blind mans road"

But like Samson I don't need my eyes to defy
strong holds
I trust Christ as my spirit's guide
Like the Israelites wid the pillar of fire
As I aspire to rise higher
The Ruach winds become my magic carpet
I'm A-Lad-In his element
Travelling heaven sent
To establish ascension
Hence...

Lano Akiwumi

1

The day drew to a close over Oakley road market. What had during the day, been a sun-kissed sky, now turned red as though blushing; after spending the day smooching with the earth's hottest star. The market, now almost deserted, was strewn with abandoned crates of apples, tomatoes and courgettes, among other items of unsold merchandise.

As the stall owners packed away, a young man strolled past them almost unnoticed, until one of them called out.

"Oi, Fela, Fela."

The young man stopped and turned to see who it was blaring out his name for the whole neighbourhood to hear. If it wasn't for his short-sightedness he would have sworn it was…

"George!" Fela looked at the man in disbelief.

The chubby figure was half jogging, half waddling as he came towards the young man. When he reached him, his cheeks had turned red and he was breathing heavily.

"What's happening, Fela?" said George, grabbing Fela's hand and pulling him into a warm hug.

"What are you doing back here, G?" asked Fela. "I thought you went back to Greece for good, so that woman could make an honest man of you, what happened?"

"Yeah, well, it's a long story Fela, one that ends in tears, and I haven't got the time or the tissue to tell it right now."

Even though George smiled as he spoke, Fela saw a hint of pain flash across his eyes.

"So I guess you can say you're back on the market then?" Fela joked, trying to lighten the mood. They both laughed.

"I see you've still got that cheeky wit," said George. "I can see you ain't changed in that department." George paused and eyed Fela inquisitively. Fela had grown a lot taller since the last time George had seen him but, apart from that, his features had not changed much. He still had the same dark thick lips (though they were now dressed with a moustache), the same bony nose and well-defined cheekbones. His eyes still had that comely brightness but as George looked into them he could see something that he did not recognise. He saw that there was something different about Fela; he seemed wiser, like he'd been through a lot since they had last seen one another. "What's been going on while I've been away?"

"To be honest, I've been away almost as long as you."

"Yeah, where did you go, did your mum finally

send you back to Nigeria? Hah, hah, hah! I remember when you would get in trouble and she would threaten to."

"Nah, I never got sent to Nigeria," Fela shifted uneasily. "I've been inside for four years."

George stared back at Fela in shock. "Don't tell me that, bruvs," the concern was evident in George's grey eyes. "What happened?"

"I got caught running scams." Fela was surprised at how much shame he felt. Fela had told many people about his time in prison, and he thought that shame was no longer an issue for him; but this was George, the man who he'd known from when he was a youngster, helping him out in the market on a Saturday. He would feel so proud when after work George would hand him a tenner and say: "Well done." This was a man he had a deep respect for, he was like an uncle to Fela. He knew George was going to lecture him.

"W-w-well what can I say." George stroked his stubble. "I know you're a wise guy and I trust you've learnt from this." He paused, as if recollecting a distant memory.

"We all make mistakes bruvs, as long as we learn never to repeat them, no one can stop our conscience from freeing us." Fela was shocked. It was strange that George never lectured him, but even stranger was the defensive tone used by him, as he spoke his words of consolation.

"Thanks, G" was all Fela could utter.

"Nah, don't mention it. Listen, I've got to get back to work, if you ever need to talk give me a buzz."

They exchanged numbers and then parted ways.

After leaving the market Fela turned onto Southbury High Street. The shopping strip wasn't quite emptied yet. It was Friday night and many of the bars were packed with revellers. Scantily clad women and testosterone fuelled men stalked the strip in a milieu of excitement.

Fela stopped to watch as two drunken men started fighting across the road from him. He tried not to laugh as one of the men took a swing for his opponent and missed, falling to the ground and pulling the other man down with him. A few people who were standing by watching, ran over and separated the two of them. Fela turned and carried on walking.

I can't believe this was once me, Fela thought. *This is actual madness.* He remembered the days when he and his friends used to terrorise the High Street. Robbing, bunnin' green (smoking marijuana) and fighting were only a few of the many atrocities they committed. And all for what, the *street fame!* They thought they would get respect and become great amongst their peers if they ran the streets. As he recalled his younger days he could not help but laugh.

He was walking down the high street quite briskly when he noticed a man coming towards him carrying a video recorder in his hands.

"Yo, bruv," said the man stopping Fela in his tracks. "Do you wanna buy a video recorder bro?" Fela looked at the man with faint recognition. He was a short dark skinned man with rough skin and cheeks that looked sucked in.

4

"Nah, I'm alright thanks," replied Fela, "Don't I know you from somewhere though?"

The man's leathery skin cracked into creases as he screwed up his face. He looked like he had some recollection but he could not quite generate enough memory to grasp it. Fela, who had also been searching his memory, finally got it.

"You were in jailhouse innit?" The man's mouth contorted into a strained smile and he nodded solemnly in response. Fela looked in his eyes. They looked vacant like the eyes of a blind man. "What's your name again?" Fela continued.

"Paul, innit." The man said, after a pause, not even looking at Fela. His eyes darted in every direction like he was watching an imaginary Ping-Pong match. Fela looked him up and down. He was wearing a sweatshirt that was torn in places and his denim jeans were dotted with stains. The video recorder he carried looked as battered and scared up as the ashy hands that held it. Every time a car passed by Paul would focus all his attention on it for a few seconds then he would go back to watching his Ping-Pong game. Fela felt uneasy.

"Anyway bro, I'm gonna bounce now, but take care of your self, yeah." Fela held out his hand to the man without thinking. The man raised his hand but Fela clenched his into a fist and…touched the man's hands lightly and departed."What's your name again mate?" Shouted the man as Fela was walking off.

"F…Philip." said Fela. He looked round but Paul was busy with the next potential customer.

Seeing Paul sent Fela's mind on a journey back

to his prison cell. Ever since his release he had tried hard to not think about prison but something always happened to remind him. Paul was his cellmate near the beginning of his sentence. It was a major problem for Fela because Paul was not the most hygienic person. He went for days without bathing and he never used to wash his hands after using the toilet. His odour repulsed Fela. It was strong like spirits and it smelt like stale corned beef. It was so bad that he asked the guards if he could be moved from the cell before he did something drastic. Unfortunately he never got his request so one day:

"Oi, Paul man go and have a shower, you're stinking up the whole cell. Look at your hair, it's got nits in it, get up!" Fela snatched a magazine out of Paul's hand.

"Give it back to me," said Paul, getting off his bed.

"Nah, go and shower—What? Who you pushing?"

THWACK!

Fela hit him over the head with the magazine. As swift as lightning Paul's fist smashed into Fela's right cheek and a fight broke out between them. The noise of the commotion aroused the interest and jeers of the neighbouring cells. They were shouting all kinds of things to hype up the situation. Suddenly the cell door opened and some prison guards burst into the cell. They all wrestled to pull Fela's hands off Paul's neck.

"Alright, break it up," one of them shouted as they peeled Fela's fingers away from Paul's neck. "And shut up the rest of you lot." The shouts from the other cells slowly subsided as Paul sat gasping for breath and Fela was led struggling out of the cell.

Fela was sentenced to a day in solitary confinement and lost all his privileges for a week. He never saw Paul again after that, the word was that he got transferred to another prison. Fela felt bad about what he had done because he knew Paul was hooked on crack to the extent where he literally could not help himself. Looking back Fela knew he had really only fought with Paul because he saw it as an easy opportunity to prove himself. It was his first time inside and Fela did not want to come across as a 'shook one', who could not 'hold it up'. The 'block', as they called it, was a tiny cell, with a little window for light, a mattress (which was taken away during the day) and graffiti all over the walls. He spent the time doing exercise, reciting his favourite lyrics, sleeping and …

"Umph!" cried Fela, coming back to reality as he bumped into someone. "Sorry."

"It's okay," the person replied. He was a short friendly looking, elderly, Negro man. "Don't worry about it young sir." Fela apologised once again then continued walking.

Coming to the traffic lights he was about to cross when he locked eyes with another man on the other side of the street. He was light skinned, fairly built with a bald head and tattooed arms. Fela was going to turn away when the man gestured with his arms as if to say "What cha looking at?" Fela, not being one to back down from a challenge, responded by shouting:

"What!" The words left his mouth before he could

even think about what he was saying, it was like an automatic reaction. The boy shouted something in return but it was drowned out by the noisy traffic, beeping at a stationary car blocking the road. At that moment Fela felt someone tapping on his shoulder and he was distracted.

"Hey there, young sir." Fela turned round to see the elderly man he had just bumped into standing behind him. The man was short with a balding head, which was grey in places. "Why are you young boys so restless?" He had a strong West Indian accent. "Can't you all learn to get along?" The man nodded in the direction of Fela's opponent, who was walking off.

"What do you mean?" said Fela indignantly. "The guy was looking at me funny, I wanted to know what his problem was. You can't be too careful out here, you don' t know whether a man's a friend or a foe!" The old man smiled, flashing a gold tooth."Well then, go find out." the old man rejoined. "Approach them and show them you're not looking any trouble from nobody and that will be the end of it." Fela shook his head and tried to interject but the old man wouldn't let him.

"Listen, nine times out of ten, they won't be looking for trouble, they're simply just reacting to the hostility of their surroundings. In other words, they are watching you because they aren't sure whether you're a friend or a foe. Tell me, if you look in the mirror and screw up your face what will you see?—A screwed up face looking straight back at you. You are all just reflections of each other."

Fela was taken aback, the old man's reasoning did make sense. "I feel what your saying, 'er Mr—."

"Mr Decent Henry," said the man, extending his arm. "But you can call me Decent."

"Fela, Fela Moore," Fela gave the man a warm handshake. "I feel what you're saying sir, Mr Decent, but it's a cold world out here and it's not everyone that is a stray sheep. 'Nuff man are wolves out to do you some harm,"—Decent listened intently—"you have to be on your guard in the concrete jungle. The streets are like prison to me, it's every man for himself and only the strong survive."

"Have you been to prison?"

"Yeah, I only got out a month ago. I did a four-year stretch but it felt like eternity, to the extent that I still don't feel free." Fela paused and looked up at the twilight sky, he gazed in envy at the birds who seemed to tease him, as they showed off their freedom to fly.

"Life is what you make it," retorted Decent. "It only becomes a prison when you allow yourself to become subject to your circumstances. Learn to love yourself unconditionally and your inner freedom will come."

They were interrupted when Fela's phone started ringing. It was his friend Ramona, who he was supposed to have linked, over an hour ago. He motioned to Decent with his finger, asking to be excused, as he hurriedly explained to Ramona that he would be with her shortly.

"Listen," Fela said after finishing on the phone. "Decent I need to go, thanks for the talk." Decent shook his hand and gave him a business card.

"That's my bookshop right there, stop by some time so we can reason, you know where this is don't you?"

"Yeah, it's near the train station, I've been past it before." Decent nodded and saluted him. Fela did likewise and went on his way.

2

Bloomsbury Estate was one of north London's most notorious areas. It was rumoured to be a criminal breeding ground, infested with drug users, dealers, ex-cons and unruly youngsters. Of course most who held this opinion had never visited the neighbourhood and so could have easily been exaggerating; nevertheless, as with many rumours, there was some truth in their report.

Police rarely ever ventured there unless they were armed and had back up. The estate had experienced it's fair share of shootouts and stabbings. However because no-one ever came forward with information, due to fear and a general feeling of hopelessness, it was difficult for the police to investigate these incidents.

The Estate was a cluster of council flats, overshadowed by two austere grey tower blocks. The two towers looked like the remains of some ancient, pagan, phallic symbols; they were worn and had been around since the seventies. The council flats were a more recent development but they also lacked any aesthetic appeal. From the outset the place looked daunting.

To Fela, who was no foreigner to the estate, there was nothing immediately terrifying about it. In fact it was like a second home to him, he had never lived on the estate but he used to hangout there with his bredrin' Shaun, who lived in one of the towers. Some of his most favourite childhood memories were spent playing one touch football on the concrete pitch. The pitch was still there, surrounded by the same steel cage just as Fela remembered it . Nothing had changed much since he had been inside. It was like a paradox, it was good to come home to the familiar but it was bad that the familiar was still a paragon of haplessness.

As Fela entered the estate he heard what sounded like gun fire and tyres screeching. He ducked behind a wall but after peering round it he realised it was just someone on a motorbike doing backfires. A convertible had pulled up alongside it and some youth were crowded round. One of the youth came riding up to Fela on a mountain bike, and as he came closer Fela recognised him.

"Wha's 'appnin Tiny?"

"Is dat you Fela?" replied the boy. He stopped the bike, pulled up his baseball cap and touched Fela's fist. "You cool blood, what's g'waning."

"Nothing much, I'm on my way to check Ramona. Who's that over there?" Fela pointed with eyes.

"Dat's Shine in the ride and Roach is on the superbike."

"Okay." Fela nodded his head in acknowledgement.

Tiny reached in his tracksuit pocket and brought out a folded piece of paper.

"Look, me and my crew made it into the local papers." he showed Fela the article. When Fela saw '**Gun crime**' he thought Tiny was in trouble but when he read on he realised Tiny had emceed at an anti-gun crime rally and the paper was 'biging' him up. As a sign of approval, Fela touched fists with him.

"This is really good little man, keep it up bro."

"I am, mans ain't stopping till we make it out here." said Tiny slowly riding off. "Later!"

"Yeah, one love." Fela turned to one of the flats and climbed to the second floor. Everyone seemed to be talking about "making it". Fela once had a dream of making it, but now that the quest for street fame was over, he needed a new direction to point his aspirations. Inside him an insatiable desire to be great was driving him crazy. Living life just surviving day to day wasn't enough, even the animals could do that.

"What sets humans a side from all other animals is our ability to influence our destiny and the destiny of others." The words of Pastor Blake echoed in his mind. They came from the tape "When destiny calls." Whilst in jail he had listened to that tape over and over again, till it snapped and his mother had to send him another copy. When he got to number 20 he stopped and knocked on the brown door.

"Who is it?" came the reply.

"It's Fela."

"Hold on." The door slowly opened and Ramona

let out a slight squeal of excitement. She grabbed hold of him in a bear hug, pressing her head into his chest.

"How are you?"

"I'm fine." He looked her up and down then pecked her on both sides of her chubby ebony cheeks. "How about yourself?"

"I'm cool," She said leading him to the living room "I've just come back from dropping Kenya at her Granny's house. She's gonna spend the week end with her."

"Oh that's a shame I was looking forward to seeing her." said Fela disappointed, then he inquired after a short pause. "How was your trip to Canada anyway?"

"It was amazing," She disappeared into the kitchen and returned with two glasses and a carton of orange juice. "I've never met such lovely people." He listened intently as she relayed to him all of her experiences from shovelling snow off her aunts front lawn to visiting some national park .

They sat and talked ecstatically, Fela found it easy to converse with her, she really took time out to listen and understand. Her frequent visits whilst he was in jail showed she was a true friend. He had known her since secondary school. Though they were good friends now it hadn't always been that way. They couldn't stand each other at one point. They were never able to figure out why, they simply just never clicked. It was only when Ramona started dating Fela's friend Shaun, in the last year of school, that they were forced to become aquatinted . As they got to know each other, they realised they had a lot in common. Peanut butter and banana sandwiches amongst other things. Now they were close friends, it was only right that Ramona made Fela, Kenya's godfather.

"Where's Calvin?" Fela inquired.

"I don't know, he might be down at the youth club, he's always there on Friday nights." She glanced at the time; it was quarter past ten. "Let me phone him quickly to find out where he is." She picked up the phone but on hearing someone at the door she put it back down again. "That must be him now, Calvin?"

Calvin appeared silently at the doorway, behind him stood a tall and slender Caucasian woman. Calvin's eye was badly bruised; he was holding an ice pack to it. Ramona rushed over to him.

"What happened to your eye Calvin?" He just walked past her silently looking vex. He went straight to his room.

"Hi, I'm Brenda Morgan, I work down at the BIG Thinking, youth project."

The woman shook hands with Ramona. "Calvin got into a fight outside the youth club on his way home. The other boys were not from the youth club and when another worker and myself came to break it up, they ran off. I thought I should bring him home just in case they were lurking somewhere, waiting for him." She said letting out an awkward laugh.

"Thank you very much?" said Ramona sincerely. "I really appreciate all that you've done."

"Don't mention it, it's my duty to look out for them. I'm gonna get going now but if you need anything, give me a call on this number." She scribbled her number down on a piece of paper and gave it to Ramona. She then bid them all farewell and left.

Fela got up to leave soon after the youth worker. He had wanted to talk to Calvin but Ramona said to leave him, he wouldn't be in the mood to talk. Fela couldn't help feeling it for Ramona. Her mother had passed away just going on two years and she was left to look after Calvin as well as raise Kenya who was barely 1 at the time. She had dealt with a lot in the 21 years she had been on this earth.

Shaun, her child's father went to jail on some drugs and firearms possession charge while she was pregnant. The stress almost caused her to miscarry. Soon after her mother passed, Calvin went off the rails. He got caught stealing car stereos and was almost sent to a detention centre. Lack of funds was another issue for her, Fela wanted to help but he didn't know how.

He meditated on Pastor Blake's words as he walked home. *If we have an ability to influence our destiny and the destiny of others*, he thought, *greatness must be measured by how many people you can positively influence.* The night was cool as he walked home, he spotted a lone star shinning in the moon light mist. Where were all the others? Obscured by pollution. It was the perfect analogy for him. He felt like a lone star amidst the polluted night life. Drunks fouled the air with profanity and the smell of booze. "Ghetto superstars" who Fela was once proud to have been associated with, drove past and he hid his face. He did not want them to see him, he did not need their hype he just wanted to be alone to think. He wanted to be great. He wanted to help improve the world he had once played a part in destroying. What would the future be like for little ones like Kenya if things didn't change? He dreaded to think of the answer. He just didn't know how he was gonna do it. The script society had given him was the bad black man role. Where was the role for the respectful black man? According to society those roles were swept away with the last century. It was no longer "cool" to be positive. In jail when he tried to reason with some brothers they told him they didn't want to hear his preaching. It seemed like society did not have a place for a man on a quest for righteousness.

He walked past the poster of a rap artist that the streets hailed as one who was "keeping it real". He was a typical thug icon, with the money, women and a crew. In his poster he stood poised with a screwed up face like the cigar in his mouth was really a lemon. The woman standing next to him wore an identical grey mink to his, except under hers she wore a bikini made of money. Fela turned away in disgust. *How can I fight against this*, he thought, *it's like it's me against the world*. He wanted to re-write the black man's script but he didn't have the means to do so. He had made some sporadic attempts at writing rap lyrics but his waves of inspiration were inconsistent. He was praying to God for some kind of miracle because he couldn't see things improving any other way. He wanted group support from some like-minded people.

By the time he got home, his mother was asleep. She left a post-it-note saying that there was some Jollof rice waiting for him in the fridge. He warmed it up and decided to write a letter to Shaun.

"Greetings King, what's the haps? I hope everything is fine. Sorry I ain't wrote to you all this time, things have been hectic since I came out. I've been looking for a job, helping my mum around the house, visiting family etc. I went to see Ramona today and she's cool. Didn't get to see Kenya, she was at your mums, I heard she is doing fine though.

Road ain't no different since we left. It's the same game the only thing that's changed is some of the players. The gun ting's getting deep though, man are buying them for next to nothing. I'm trying to distance myself from all of that, being another statistic is long! There comes a time when a man has to grow up and stand on his own two, without stumbling into foolishness. My life's purpose is deeper than all of that, I just know it. I wanna set things up so when you touch road we can both eat off a clean plate, you know, legit. I don't know what I'm gonna do but rest assured I'm gonna do something soon. Till then hold your head up soldier.

+God bless+ from your truest comrade,
Fela Moore"

3

After some tedious searching Fela was able to secure a job down at a local warehouse, this in theory was his first job. That's excluding the time he worked for a Fast Food restaurant which only lasted two hours. Being shouted at by a short Chinese woman, in a smoky kitchen, amidst a bunch of foreigners he couldn't understand, was not the way he envisioned earning a living--so he quit.

The warehouse job wasn't that desirable either. It was run like a dictatorship and the work they were dishing out, was like slave labour. The place was a store house for a major furniture retailer, so Fela had to count stock and move stock. It sounded easy when Fela read the job description, but when it came down to it, the amount of stock he had to manage in such a short space of time was too much. The dictator, Mr Platt, was an East End gangster wannabe who, when he spoke, exaggerated the cockney accent. He made Fela dust shelves that didn't need dusting and sweep the floor which wasn't even written in his job mandate for him to do. Fela just needed the money so he stuck at it.

The rest of the workers were mostly middle aged white men who Fela found hard to relate with. There were two younger men, a Ghanaian and Irish man, but they worked on the delivery vans so he hardly saw them. The job drained Fela both physically and spiritually. Mr Platt's attitude made it harder for him to be enthusiastic about going to work. He figured that this was why he had been late two days in a row. Fela stood at the bus stop on what was looking like his lateness hat trick. This time he had started out early but the bus had decided to be like a British summer and come late.

Fela wasn't looking at anything in particular when he noticed the youth worker that followed Calvin home, coming towards him. She stopped at the bus stop but didn't recognise him, so he pulled off his hood and went over to her.

"Hi," Fela tried to sound as pleasant as his current mood permitted. It must have been enough because she, smiled even though she looked bewildered. "I was at Calvin's house when you brought him home the other day." said Fela, sincerely.

"Oh yes I remember you, Brenda Morgan, and your name is?" Fela shook her hand and told her his name. "How is he, I haven't seen him at the club since?"

"He's alright, the black eye's clearing up, it wasn't too serious." Fela paused then continued. "He isn't telling us what it was about. I just hope he isn't planning some kind of revenge attack."

"He'll come round, he's more sensible than that. Just give him sometime you'll see."

The bus slowly came into sight. Fela thought it was trying to make him late on purpose.

"I wanna thank you for what you did. It was really brave of you." Fela rejoined as they climbed on to the bus.

"Aw', someone's got to do it, I want the young people to feel safe and secure while they're in my care. I do for them what I would want a youth worker to do for my kids. Also being aware of Calvin's history and how his mother's death effected him, I feel for him. He's a good kid, it would be a shame all that went to waste." The bus jerked and Fela almost fell on top of an elderly lady he was standing in front of. He apologised and continued his conversation with Brenda. He had an idea in his mind.

"We need more youth workers with a true passion like you. It's actually the sort of work I'm interested in doing."

"Why don't you?"

"No one will hire me. I have no experience and I've got a jail record."

Brenda paused thoughtfully. "Was the crime you went down for of a violent nature?"

"No, it was fraud."

Brenda did some fast calculations in her head.

"I might be able to take you on, it won't be paid though. It will have to be on a voluntary basis until our funds can cater for a new member of staff."

"But I need paid work, I can't afford to work for free." said Fela, matter-of- factly.

"You can still do your part-time work and do the voluntary stuff on the side."

Brenda picked up her bags in preparation to get off at the next stop. "At least that way you can get experience. Voluntary work always looks good on a C.V. and it will show you have previous training." Fela looked undecided, his eyebrows came together and his forehead broke into ripples as he tried to sum up Brenda's offer. The bus finally arrived at her stop and Brenda got off.

"Just think about it ok."

"Yeah." said Fela though he doubted he would.

Fela Moore rushed into the Warehouse 10 minutes late. They were having a team meeting, Mr Platt had them all lined up against the wall like criminals waiting to be executed by a firing squad. All heads turned as if on cue when Fela walked through the door.

"And look at what the cat just dragged in. Why are you late?" Fela attempted to explain but Mr Platt cut him off, as if the question he posed was rhetorical. "I don't want to hear your sorry excuses, just stand over there, I'll deal with you in a minute."

Mr Platt then went on to school the team on what was proper employee conduct. He made a point of publicly reprimanding Fela for his "sluggish" attitude to work. Once he was through with speaking to the team he released them to their tasks and called Fela into his office.

It was a cramped up space with papers and folders

all over the place. Mr Platt took a seat and rummaged through a heap of papers. When he found what he was looking for, he took a sip from a mug, and looked up at Fela.

"How long have you been with us Fela?"

"I don't, know about two weeks or so." Fela replied shrugging his shoulders.

"Two weeks exactly today, and in that time you've been late three times in a row with no feasible excuse. You come back late from lunch and I've had to speak to you on several occasions about your pace of work. It's really not acceptable." He paused to sip whatever it was he had in his mug. Fela seized this opportunity to speak.

"Mr Platt with all due respect, I feel like you're not being totally fair here. The reason why my attitude to work here is not up to scratch is because I feel uncomfortable. I'm constantly under scrutiny, which makes me feel tense and uneasy." said Fela trying to reason with him.

"So are you saying that the way we're treating you is adversely affecting your work here?" asked Mr Platt looking down at some papers.

Fela replied in the affirmative.

"So you're admitting you have a problem with your work, which I say is the reason why I keep you under my watchful eye." He lifted up a piece of paper to his eyes. "On your application form it says that you went to jail on conviction for fraud." Fela eyed him suspiciously, Mr Platt met his gaze then looked away. "After verification with the police we found out you never declared the fact that you were convicted of a robbery as well as that."

It was a cautionary sentence for robbery when Fela was fourteen. The police told him his record would be wiped clean after two years. He didn't think he still needed to declare it. He could see Mr Platt was bent on his ostracism and was looking for anything to use against him. Fela felt his blood temperature begin to rise.

"It was a caution for a minor robbery," said Fela raising his voice. "the police told me that after 2 years it would be wiped off my record, so I thought I didn't have to declare it." Fela's eyes were now set ablaze with indignation and his tone became fiery and defensive. The room was heating up.

"Now listen here, *son shine*!" said Mr Platt edging forward, his tone was subtly menacing but the fullness of his fury was barred behind his gritted teeth. His face slowly turned red like the rings on an electrical cooker. "Don't you dare, ever, *ever*, raise your voice in my office again, who do you think you are? I run this ship not you. How dare you?—" Mr Platt paused for a second and sized Fela up and down with his eyes. "You know what, get out of my office!"

Fela stood there as if rooted to the spot. He felt his fists slowly clenching together and rage bubbled up inside him like a volcano about to erupt.

"What?" said Mr Platt, looking up from the papers he had returned to reading. He fixed his cold grey eyes on Fela and they stared at one another like two pitbulls about to tear each other up. Then came a knock at the door.

Mr Platt gave Fela a mocking smirk then turned to the door.

"Come in." The doorknob turned and the intruder entered. He was a short Caucasian man with receding, brown hair, glasses and a beard. Fela recognised him to be John Forrest, Mr Platt's line-manger. He had a weird presence, it was not cold but at the same time he was not friendly, rather he had an air of someone who is always preoccupied with more important things.

"Hi, John." said Mr Platt sounding a little embarrassed. Fela gave him one last dirty look then left. If it had not been for the intrusion, Fela was sure he would have really taught Mr Platt a thing or two – with his fists. In hindsight he was glad that he never because he figured, that is exactly what Mr Platt would have wanted, for him to loose his temper and do something stupid then he would have done him for A.B.H. Then it would have been back to jail for him, for violating the terms of his probation.

He walked out of the office and marched straight off the premises without looking back. *I don't need their money,* he thought to himself, *I'll find another way to make it.*

As Fela walked down the street he felt his phone vibrating.

"Hello?"

"Oga." There was only one person that referred to him using the Nigerian variant of Mr and that was his cousin Ade. He had been in Nigeria for a month on holiday.

"When did you get back?"

"Just this morning, I've been asleep since. Where are you? Didn't you go to work today?"

"I quit that joke of a job." said Fela flatly.

"What! Why?"

"It's a long story but if you're not doing anything I'll meet you at your gates and tell you." They agreed to do that and Fela made his way to Ade's house.

Ade, a bachelor, lived in a more prestigious part of north London. His job as a computer engineer paid well. He had come far since he arrived from Nigeria to study in his late teens. Now over a decade later, his many professional accolades were opening doors on levels he didn't even know existed. Gone were his days of masterminding scam operations, he was straight legit. He regretted those days though, not only had he committed some execrable crimes, he had also got his cousin involved. When he changed and became a Christian, he tried to bring Fela with him but to no avail. It took a court case, prayer and divine intervention to achieve that.

"C-O-U-S-I-N!" Ade gave Fela a brotherly hug. He walked him into his spacious living room. As they dialogued the air was charged with elation. Fela was actually able to relay his experience at work with a sense of humour. Ade had a way of drawing the humour out of from some of the most unpleasant circumstances.

"You said his name was Mr Platt are you sure it wasn't Mr Pratt, cause hedefinitely sounded like one?"

They laughed even though the joke wasn't that good. It was only made to ease any tension Fela had.

"Life's a joke that isn't funny, just as things started looking up for me they decided to take a turn for the worst." Fela complained in jest. "Fate does definitely have a sense of irony." 'Life's a joke that isn't funny!' was Fela's favourite saying, and whenever he said it Ade always laughed.

Fela told Ade about the offer he got from Brenda, the youth worker.

"You should try it out and look for something else to do in the meantime. Do one of them New Deal courses or something. It won't be long before you get enough youth work experience to get paid work." Ade took off his glasses to clean them with his vest.

"So how's the Mother land?" inquired Fela as Ade put his glasses back on.

"It's advancing, the quality of living has definitely improved. We still haven't managed to master the art of driving on the right side of the road, but we'll get there!" They both bubbled with laughter. "But on a serious level, Nigeria has got it together when it comes to having a visible form of godliness. I felt really close to God over there. It was so humbling to see the way people were praising God even though they were living in poverty. Us Westerners have become lukewarm when it comes to God because our way of living is easy. If one has money problems, instead of seeking the Almighty, they would seek a loan shark. Another may want to know what the future holds so they consult the star signs instead of the Holy Spirit. People would argue that they will only put their faith in what they can see. They contradict themselves though, cause they believe in air even though they can't see it."

Fela listened earnestly as his cousin expounded his political and theological ideas. It wasn't the first time he had heard it, but the more he heard it the more he understood.

"Look Fela," Ade continued, "the West is set up to create a godless society, where man is a law onto himself. Instead of people following the laws of God, they are told by the so called 'intellectuals', that God does not exist. They are encouraged to make their own laws and so it becomes a case of the blind leading the blind."

"Yeah," said Fela, nodding his head. "The attitude is, if it works for me then I'm gonna do it. What people are saying really is that it's every man for himself."

4

Calvin's eye had almost cleared up. He was still wearing sunglasses though, they were designer frames so why not. They were Ramona's old pair and she let him "borrow" them. Yeah right, Calvin wasn't giving them back. He had wanted to get his hands on those shades since the time Shaun had first bought them for her. She never let him borrow them up until then, which made Calvin think that maybe good can come from a bad situation.

He wanted revenge for what they did to him. He really wanted to make Marcus and his boys pay. The beef started over a football match. Calvin's school played Marcus' school in a friendly and they almost got into a fight over fouling. Marcus claimed Calvin tripped and barged him on purpose therefore he'd wanted to fight. Before they could get into it they were parted. It was by chance that Marcus bumped into Calvin outside the youth club, Marcus was with his boys but Calvin was on his own. Ever since then he had been walking with a knife. *Next time*, he thought, *I'll be prepared for them.*

It was a Saturday afternoon, two weeks after he got jumped and Calvin was on his way to the grocery shop. His sister had sent him out to buy some milk. As he walked he noticed a group of boys riding past on mountain bikes. His heart started beating fast when he realised one of them was non other than – Marcus. One of the boys spotted him and called it to the attention of the rest of the gang. Calvin stopped where he was standing. His first impulse was to run but his pride wouldn't let him, he didn't want to look like a coward and besides they were on mountain bikes, he couldn't out run them. They slowed down as they turned and rode up to him shouting expletives, Calvin just stood there silently.

In turn, each climbed off his bike. Marcus was a little taller than Calvin and more robust. His yellowish chubby face was fitted with two slit-like eyes that projected a wonton thirst for trouble. As Marcus and his boys came towards him,

Calvin without thinking, flicked out his blade and gestured with it as if to say "come any closer and you're getting it." The boy's, not taking him seriously, just laughed and continued advancing upon him, so Calvin began waving the knife in the air like he was gonna stab them. The gang moved back.

A man driving past in a convertible pulled up in the middle of the road and ran over to them shouting.

"Oi, Oi it's Shine!" One of the boys shouted as the

man came nearer. They all looked around including Calvin.

"I hope you're not troubling my little bredrin here." Shine went over to Calvin and put his arm on his shoulder. Calvin found it hard to fight back a smug smile, especially when he saw the look of fear that crossed the faces of his adversaries.

"When I ask a question it means I want an answer, now if you don't want me to beat it out of you, speak to me." The boys mumbled some kind of denial but Calvin wasn't having none of it. He explained to Shine what had transpired. The boys began to argue with him and amongst themselves.

"All right," Shine's deep, husky voice subdued everyone else's. "Alright this is what we're gonna do. I want Calvin to give Marcus a punch in the face and then that's it. Everyone's even." Marcus knew he had no other choice so he agreed. Calvin swung for him but Marcus moved so he only clipped him. Shine allowed Calvin another shot and he punched his rival square in the nose. Marcus held his face and dropped down to the ground.

"Alright the beef is squashed, come little man." He motioned to Calvin to follow him. They walked over to Shines ride. He was a big, tall dark skinned negro with a peculiar walk and yellow eyes. He looked thirty odd, although he was only in his late twenties. His skin was rough like bark and he had a brutish demeanour, yet he carried a charm that was quite becoming of him. The way he conducted himself commanded attention and respect.

"Your Tiny's boy innit, the one that got me the car stereo that time." Calvin nodded and replied in the affirmative. Shine opened the door for him. Calvin felt excitement rush through his body, here he was sitting in the ride of the most respected and revered street soldier about. Shine started up the car with a pensive look on his face.

"I've been meaning to get at you." He continued. "I've got a business proposition for you. I need someone to control my weed line for me and Tiny recommended you because you know all the buyers round here. Is that correct?"

"Yeah, I know a couple." said Calvin coyly. Shine reached in his glove compartment and brought out a wad of cash. Before he shut it Calvin saw the nozzle of a gun under some papers.

"Here," Shine didn't even count it he just handed the notes to him. "Take that for now, it's a little introductory gift. I'm gonna holler at you with the line and the food later on."

Calvin couldn't think straight. Bedazzled by the man's charisma and the amount of money he had in his hand, Calvin agreed to meet Shine at the appointed time. He got out of the ride street dreaming. He was so caught up that he didn't even feel the vibration of his phone. An enraged Ramona had been calling him to find out where he was with her milk. As far as he was concerned working for Shine would bring money, power and respect. He had nothing to worry about.

5

"… So King Nebucadnezzar erected this gold image and commanded everyone in the Kingdom of Babylon to worship it. But Shadrach, Meshach and Abednego refused to do it. They didn't care about the consequences, they weren't gonna let anyone or anything come between them and their God. Now Church I want you to get this, we are living in a modern day Babylon and money is the new idol we are being encouraged to worship. How many know that money has become the god of this world. As the famous saying goes "Money makes the world go round." Now in the mist of this dire crisis we're in, how many realise they are being called to leadership, that God is looking for men and women like Shadrach, Meshach and Abednego, who will stand up and be counted. Men and women who are not willing to conform no matter what the consequence may be. Who will go against all odds to do what's right no matter what the crowd is doing or saying…"

Fela Moore sat in the back row of the sparsely

packed auditorium, listening to Pastor Blake break down his theology. Ever since he had come out of jail he had been putting off coming to church. Every time his mum asked him to come he turned her down. He liked to lie in on Sundays and plus he found the whole church affair rather tiresome. He had come on this occasion to stop his mum from complaining and also because he did wanted to meet Pastor Blake. To his surprise he actually liked it, the way the sermon was delivered was really interesting. Pastor Blake used humour and relevant facts to get his points across. He had come in late but it wasn't hard for him to catch on to what was being said. After the service Fela went over to his mum.

"I see you managed to make it then." She said half jokingly, giving him a mock clip round the ear. Fela dodged it laughing, his mum was always extra bubbly after church. She went around introducing him to some of her friends in the congregation, who could not believe she had a son of his age. It was understandable, even though Lola was forty-four, she had managed to retain the down-to-earth realism and the unquenchable zest for life that is only characteristic in young children. Youthful freshness permeated through her every fibre giving her a natural glow that adorned her with beauty and made her look younger than she really was. Fela looked a lot like his mother, they had the same eyes and lips, and many of Fela's facial expressions resembled his mother's. All Fela needed to do was shave his moustache, get an eighties gericurl, some hooped earrings and people might just mistake them for sisters!

"Listen you, the Pastor and his family have invited us to his house this afternoon and I want us to go." Though her tone sounded causal, Fela knew his mum was serious.

"Yeah I can make that, what time?"

She said that the aim was to be there for 4pm. The time was 1pm, which gave him time to go home and write some lyrics. He had planned to the use whole day for writing but, for his mum he would have to make a sacrifice. His mum had made plenty for him, especially after his dad left.

It happened when he was 7, his mum first told him his dad had gone on holiday, maybe even she never thought it was a permanent arrangement. One night he heard his mum crying so he went into her room and she told him everything. He was so upset that his mum kept him home the next day. He grew up resenting his dad for leaving them, especially when he found out it was for another woman. Ever since then it was just him and his mum. His cousin, Ade, was there but he never lived with him.

"Is Ade coming?" inquired Fela.

"Yeah he's gonna pick us up after his Church finishes." came the reply.

When Fela got home he started writing almost straight away. What the pastor said during the service had inspired him. He called the piece "Stand up", the basic concept was that all the true soldiers should stand up and be counted. He had been writing almost every day since he landed back on road and he was beginning to find himself on paper. He was beginning to define his style.

When Ade arrived he had almost completed the piece but his mother had a way of being very persuasive. She repeatedly knocked on his door until he could concentrate no longer, so he gave in and obliged her request to "find his self downstairs straight away!"

When they arrived a cheerful Pastor Blake, greeted them taking off his oven gloves. He was wearing a T-shirt, jeans and sandals. Out of his suit he looked like a regular brother.

"Your mum's told me a lot about you. It's finally good to meet you in the flesh." He was shaking Fela's hand as he spoke and straight away Fela felt an instant connection with him.

"Likewise, it's good to finally put a face to the phrase 'Christianity is like a nail the more people knock it, the deeper it goes.' It kept me going when people tried to rubbish my faith in jail."

"We thank God, for allowing me to be of service." Replied the pastor, chuckling as he led them into the dining room. A young woman was placing cutlery around the glass table. She had her hair out natural in baby locks, her skin was like smooth ebony but yet in all her appeal there was nothing glossy about her. Fela was immediately taken aback by her beauty. She turned as they entered the room and they both meet each others gaze. When Fela had an opportunity to look back on that moment he could not decide if he imagined it but was sure he saw her eyes sparkle.

Whether they did or not, looking in her eyes definitely made the wings of his heart flutter.

"Fela this is my daughter Sapphire, Sapphire meet Fela." said the pastor. They shook hands briefly. Sapphire then went to embrace Fela's mother who she was already aquatinted with. She then hugged Ade who she was also no stranger to. At that moment an older woman came through the door, with a warm smile she shook hands with Fela introducing her self as the pastor's wife. She looked like the older version of Sapphire except that her hair was in long braids and she was slightly shorter.

After the general greetings were out of the way it was time to eat. The meal served was the Sunday traditional; roast potatoes, turkey and an assortment of vegetables drenched in some fine gravy. As they ate, the party conversed genially, discussing various topics ranging from politics to music. Once the food was finished and dessert was on it's way, the Pastor in an effort to build a rapport with Fela, challenged him to a game of chess while the rest went to catch a movie.

"So your mother tells me you're into poetry." The pastor commented as he arranged the pieces on the board. He was a man in his late forties, average height but with broad shoulders and thick arms. He wore a neatly trimmed goatee, and he had a full head of hair, though his hair was greying in places. His expression was one of someone who was cheerful and friendly but knew when it was time to be serious.

"Yeah I write a little. Been doing it for 3 years now,

on and off." Fela's mind was distracted as he spoke to the pastor. The game had started and he was more focused on the threat posed by the pastors queen.

"Do you perform your stuff or is it too personal for that?"

"I don't mind performing as long as it's in front of the right crowd. Why, do you know of anything?" The pastor pondered briefly then moved his queen from the dangerous position it was in. Fela had set a trap for it.

"Well it's just that in a few weeks the church is hosting a charity event. People will be bringing in things they no longer want like clothes, old computers, and books amongst other things. They will then be shipped over to India."

"What, you're shipping people to India?" asked Fela with a cheeky grin, they both laughed.

"If only," replied the pastor. "No, the items contributed will be shipped out. We've been doing this since last year, when we shipped some stuff over to West Africa."

"So where do I come into it, do you want me to perform?"

"Yeah, we would like that if you don't have a problem with that."

"No it will be no problem at all," Fela moved his bishop to take one of the pastor's knights. "Let me know the date and I'll be there."

"I will do just that. Now you might want to consider re-making your last move unless throwing me your queen like that is part of some abstract strategy you have up your sleeve." Fela looked at the board and let out a cry of utter disbelief, he had made the wrong move. Although the Pastor gave him chance to re-make the move Fela opted for the game to continue, he didn't want his "professionalism compromised".

As they played Fela heard the sound of someone coming down the stairs hurriedly. The person then burst into the room suddenly. Fela and the Pastor looked up.

"Oh so you've finally decided to join us Warren, did you have a nice sleep?" the Pastor's tone was almost sarcastic.

"I was up making beats all night again, you know how I do." He spoke with a northern accent. Even though he was dialoguing with the pastor he was staring at Fela with a look of faint recognition, Fela returned his gaze with the same expression.

He knew the man's face from somewhere but he couldn't recall where from. Warren turned to look at the pastor.

"Yeah I know we could hear you." continued the pastor, making his move on the board. He looked up and introduced Warren as his nephew, they shook hands without much fervour. Fela was still trying to figure out where he had seen the brother before. Then it came to him in a flash as Warren turned around to leave the room. It was then that Fela spotted the tattoo on his right arm, it was then that Fela realised this was the boy who was trying to stare him out the other day on the high road.

Fela continued playing the game of chess somewhat

distracted by his revelation of who Warren was. *The world's too small* was all he could think to himself. Due to Fela's lack of concentration he was outwitted by the pastor and he lost the game of chess. As much as Fela was upset over the rash move he made he gave himself props for lasting so long. He wanted to play him again but it was getting late and he promised Ramona he would stop by hers. He wanted to leave right after he used the toilet. Following the pastor's direction's he found his way upstairs to the second floor of the three-storey house. As he climbed to the top of the stair case he came face to face with Warren, he had a towel in his hand.

"Where's the toilet bro?" asked Fela just trying to ease the tension.

"Right over there." Warren pointed in the direction he was heading in. Fela thanked him and went in to relieve himself. When he came out Warren was still standing there obviously waiting to use the shower that was in the bathroom. Fela felt it was the perfect time to make his peace with the young man.

"It's Warren innit," Fela started. Warren nodded his head wearily. "I don't know if you remember me but I think there was a misunderstanding between us on Southbury Road the other day. I feel like it might have been mostly my fault and I just wanted to apologise for any disrespect on my behalf." He extended his arm and Warren returned the gesture.

"We were giving each other the evil eye innit?" asked Warren. Fela affirmed the statement with a slow nod.

"Yeah I remember that, it's cool G, I'm not watching that. To be honest I thought you were someone else. You look like someone I had beef with in the jailhouse but thinking about it he was alot shorter than you and he had a missing finger. Now unless you got hold of some growth tonic that made you shoot up and sprout a new pinkie finger you couldn't possibly be him." They both laughed in chorus.

"You never know cause I have been to jail." chuckled Fela. Warren asked him when he forfeited his freedom. They were in jail at different times but they talked about it like they experienced it together. They conversed like two old friends. Fela found out that Warren was originally from Manchester's troubled Moss side district. He had moved down to London to start afresh, he was too deep in the grind up there and he needed a clean break away from it all. His mum thought it would be good for him to go and stay with her brother, who was Pastor Blake. Warren was trying to pursue a career in music production and becoming a DJ.

They went into his room to look at his equipment and play some beats. The room was in a mess, clothes were strewn all over the place and there were boxes stacked up against the wall. Warren walked over to his desk and turned on the computer it was supporting. After a few clicks of the mouse Warren had some beats running, Fela was impressed, the beats were better than he expected. He started rhyming to what he was hearing.

"Wait, wait run that by me again." Warren was

equally impressed with Fela's rhyming ability. He restarted the track and let Fela do his thing.

"You're tight man, how long you been spitting for?" asked Warren. Fela told him it had been three years. From here Fela started telling Warren about his plans to make it big, but just as he started getting into it he remembered he had promised to stop by Ramona's before it got too late so he could get to see Kenya while she was still awake.

"Warren I'm sorry to cut our convo short but I need to go and check my goddaughter before it gets too late. God willing we'll meet up and discuss things on another occasion" He touched fists with him and started going towards the stairs.

✦   ✦   ✦

"... Stop lying to me Calvin, we've both just read the letter, your tutor's saying you've been playing truant. Now I want the truth, why haven't you been going to school?" Ramona's voice resounded down the musty hallway as Fela walked to her door. He had thoughts of turning back; he didn't want to make things more awkward than they already were. The door suddenly burst open and Calvin came charging out, Ramona came out after him.

"Where do you think you're going?" she said grabbing his jacket.

"Come off me!" retorted Calvin, giving her a violent shrug that made her fall back to the floor, Fela rushed over to help her up. To his surprise Kenya was at her mother's side bawling her eyes out, he hadn't even noticed when she had come out. He tried to console her whilst helping her mum up. Once Ramona was on her feet she started after Calvin, who was escaping down the stairs. She was like a charging bull pursuing it's tormentor. Fela picked up Kenya and ran after Ramona. When he got outside she was shouting threats after Calvin, who was seated in the passenger side of a convertible, making a clean get away.

Fela reached his yard late that night, he had spent hours trying to console Ramona who broke down shortly after the whole incident. She felt like she had the weight of the world on her shoulders and it was too much to bare.

"I can't do this anymore." she said putting her face in her hands. "I just can't deal with the stress." She then went on to list her problems which ranged from being a single parent to the misadventures of Calvin and to top it all off a baby father locked down. This was a different side to her that Fela wasn't used to. Why--of course, he had seen her low before but never had it come to the point where she wanted to give up. He felt helpless, everything that he said just seemed like a "you're just saying that to make me feel better" statement. After a long silence that felt like eternity she asked him to do something he was not expecting.

"Fela can you pray for me?" In all the years he had known her she had never once shown any real interest in God. Sometimes the way she carried on made him wonder whether she even believed in the Almighty. It was a shock to his system and after he had indulged

43

her, he made a point of asking her why she had made such a request.

"From when we were young, mum used to always pray for us when we went to her with our problems. From headaches caused by bumps on the head to ones caused by emotionally retarded boyfriends she was always ready to say a prayer for you." She smiled musing at the memories as they flashed before her eyes. Kenya by now had fallen asleep on her lap, she picked her up and went to put her to sleep. She returned a few minutes later wiping tears from her eyes.

"You know just looking at my baby in there—." she paused to wipe her eyes. "Just looking at her and how sweet and innocent she is, made me realise that it's my duty to shelter her from harm. On her deathbed my mum was trying to speak to me and through her oxygen mask it sounded like she was saying, 'Take care of everyone for me.' I told her I would, and I have to honour my word. Even though Calvin gets me vex I wouldn't be able to forgive myself if anything bad was to happen to him." She paused as if she was lost in thought.

"But don't try and do it on your own Ramona, you know I'm always here for you. Plus my mum said whenever you want you can drop Kenya off at ours, she'll be happy to baby-sit for you." Fela got up, he was ready to leave, he was gonna do some early morning writing the next day and he needed to sleep. Ramona thanked him for all his help and saw him to the door.

"Tell your mum that I'm gonna stop round sometime tomorrow to drop off her birthday present."

she shouted after him. Her words took some time to sink in, then it hit, so hard that he almost fell down the stairs. Birthday present! Fela slapped his head in disbelief. How could he have forgotten, the next day was the 20th of May, his mum's birthday. He hadn't planned or bought anything, he went home in a state of panic.

6

Fela awoke early the next day and made his mum some breakfast in bed. He knew what he was gonna do for her birthday, he would take her to a restaurant that Friday. He knew one not too far from where they lived that served some off the best Thai food. His mother received the breakfast heartily and he told her about the plans for the restaurant.

"I'm thinking about inviting Ade and maybe Ramona."

"Yeah, that's ok with me as long as it's not going to be too expensive." His mother replied. "You know your not working so you don't want to overdo it." It was going to be a big expense for him but he planned to borrow money from Ade. He deeply regretted going on a shopping spree with the little money he had saved whilst working. He had needed some new outfits but they didn't necessarily need to be designers, he called it a bad habit; Ade called it a rich habit.

"Its alright, I should have it covered." He said assuredly.

After his mother had left for work, he tried to do some writing but nothing was coming out, so he decided to go for a walk. He circled the bookshop that Decent owned in search of some inspiring conversation and books to stimulate his brain. The shop was down a side street. 'Cornerstone books' was written across the top of the small store. He had passed it on numerous occasions when he was younger but back then reading didn't interest him. The only print he was interested in reading then was the type that appeared on bank statements.

"Ah my friend." Decent held out his hand as he approached Fela, from behind the counter. "How are you Fela?"

"I'm fine what about yourself?" Fela felt embarrassed, the man remembered his name but he struggled to show the same level of respect. They shook hands and Decent asked him what had brought him to the shop.

"I'm looking for some new books to stimulate my brain and maybe something for mumsy as well, it's her B-day today." He looked around as he talked, there were shelves packed with numerous titles as well as video's. "I didn't know you did video's as well ... Decent." The name just came to him out of nowhere.

"It's there on the card." Admittedly Fela hadn't looked at the card so he couldn't say anything but "Oh". "We do books, video's, CD's and tapes." Decent said pointing out items he'd recommend. Fela picked a book of Martin Luther King's sermons, and a book of poetry for himself. For his mum he bought a motivational tape featuring a popular Christian speaker and a Naija (Nigerian) movie.

"So how is everything with you?" Inquired Decent, putting Fela's purchase in a bag. "Does the world still seem like a prison to you?" Fela nodded his head.

"I feel trapped behind the bars of poverty." Fela explained as he told Decent how he quit his job . "I feel like a runaway slave. I've left the plantation with no money and nowhere to go. I feel to just turn back and go work on the plantation. At least that way I can have the means to buy my provisions." He let out a sigh and shook his head. "To make it in this world it seems like you have to sell your soul."

The old man looked concerned. "So let me get this right, you feel trapped because you don't have any money?" Fela nodded. "So do you believe personal freedom and money are synonymous? Do you believe that in order to have freedom you need money?"

"Nah that's not what I mean." replied Fela "It just seems like everything I try goes wrong. I've got no career and no definite direction I want to go in. I'm a big man and I still have to borrow money from people. I don't know where my life is going, I feel trapped because every day it's the same old same old, my life ain't improving and it's depressing. The world's changing so fast and I feel like I've been left behind."

At this point a customer, walked into the shop and came up to the counter. He was a clean-shaven Caucasian with a cleft in his chin and a sharp nose, dressed modestly in a white T-shirt and army fatigues. Decent put their convo on pause and greeted the man, with a welcoming handshake. He called him by the name, Scott, so Fela figured they were aquatinted. The man then turned to Fela and introduced himself and Fela did likewise. He asked for the books he'd pre-ordered and Decent pulled out two books from behind the counter. Fela read the titles, one was a book on Black history and the other was an analysis of contemporary Black culture. As soon as the man had paid for the books he said he had to dash, shook both their hands and left the shop hurriedly.

"That is one hardworking guy, I don't know how he does it." Decent said laughing to himself. "Just watching him can make one tired." He then went on to explain who Scott was. He was a local journalist who had a passion for the community and working towards a better society on the whole. Not only had he published a book of politically charged essays, he was also part of the steering group for a local community initiative called Big Thinking. The name sounded familiar to Fela but he couldn't remember where he had heard it before.

"He's been coming to this shop for years to buy books." Explained Decent. "I was shocked by his interest in the social problems which face Nubians at first, so I asked him about it. He simply told me he hated injustice and wanted to do all that was in his power to stop it. He says his basic motto is "do unto others just as you want done to your self." Decent then explained to him how Scott had been on missions to India, Africa and Brazil. Fela felt inspired, this sounded like a man who was trying to take control of his destiny, whilst positively influencing the destines of others. This is what he wanted to do, but he didn't know how to.

"He's actually a good person to link up with. He attends a community forum, which meets every fortnight; it would be good for you to check it out. I'll give you the details before you leave, but as for you feeling imprisoned I can relate to that because believe it or not I felt like that at one point in my life." He wiped his brow with a hanky.

"It's a feeling of unfulfillment, it comes when you haven't been able to define what your purpose is. You spoke of making it but what does that mean."

Fela played with the hairs on his chin meditatively.

"I don't know, I used to think it was having money, power and respect but now I know those three won't guarantee me a secure life. I'll always be watching my back and the physical pleasures they bring don't last. I need something that will bring me inner peace, I feel like there's a war going on inside me; I'm trying to live a righteous and peaceful life in a world of strife and shallow indulgences. It's like trying to find light in darkness.

"So your purpose is to be righteous and peaceful?" Asked Decent. Fela nodded. "So you know your purpose, it seems like your problem is not knowing exactly how to maintain an inner sense of righteousness and peace."

" I guess so." Fela replied.

7

After his talk with Decent the next day Fela was in a state of perplexity. He couldn't figure out how to achieve his purpose. He believed that God had a plan for everyone's life but he didn't know how to manifest his. He felt like there were too many distractions and temptations to stop him finding out how to achieve his life's mission. The 9-5 program seemed to him like a way to keep people in a rat race for ever moving but never getting closer to their true purpose. He tried to reason out a way to achieve godliness in his mind but he couldn't, he needed advice. He decided to holler at his cousin, he was a man who seemed to work with a different sort of inspiration. He was always happy no matter what his situation, and he always had a personal goal to work towards.

He met him at a local snooker hall, in the evening after Ade finished from work. The place was dimly lit and smokey, all types of shady characters, came in and out. Fela nodded to some familiar faces and shook his head at those not so familiar ones who were offering herb. It was only because Fela knew the manger of the place that he went there to play pool. It was owned by a Greek, one of George's friends. Fela had been going there from way back. He hadn't played pool for a little while so he was a little rusty; this proved not to be a problem seeing as most of Ade's shots sent balls rebounding around the table, instead of in the pockets.

"So you find it hard to balance your spiritual needs with your physical needs?"

Ade was checking that he understood where Fela was coming from.

"Yeah," confirmed Fela. "I feel like I'm living just to satisfy my basic needs; food, clothes and shelter. I know my life has got to be about more than that, I feel like I'm meant to be great, but to do that I need to expand my circle of influence. I want to spread righteousness and peace but I'm finding hard to keep hold of them myself." Ade took a shot and accidentally potted one of Fela's balls. Fela burst out laughing.

"You were distracting me." Ade complained, unconvincingly.

"I can honestly say that you have more control over your spiritual life than you do over the pool cue." Laughed Fela as Ade feigned an expression of mock vexation. "Seriously I have little control over my spiritual growth I feel like I'm not growing." "The only reason why I'm growing and why I feel fulfilled is because I set myself goals and I reach them. All that I do is geared towards one objective and that is to spread the love of God. In order to do that I need to accept

God's love and learn to love myself unconditionally, knowing that my life in it's self is a blessing to this earth from God. Once I have the love inside me it naturally permeates through all my words and actions." Ade let out a shout of joy as he potted two balls at once but then the white followed them so it was Fela's two shots.

"So you're saying I need to work on myself first, I need to get the love of God in my life first?" Asked Fela.

"Yeah, a forest fire can be started by one tiny spark, it takes one dedicated person to start a revolution. The revolution we're dealing with is one of the mind, but how can you lead others in the right direction if you can't take yourself there? The greatest conquer is the one that can conquer himself. On our own this is impossible but with the help of the Father we can do anything." Ade chalked up his stick as he talked, Fela saw his eyes were ablaze, even though it was dark. Fela asked him what his plans were.

"I've been thinking deep about that lately. I want to impact society in such a way that people all over the earth will praise God for having made a brother like me. I want the praise to be echoing through the halls of fame long after I'm gone. It's not for my benefit, what can man give me that God can't? I just want to be a vessel for the Father to manifest His power through. I want God to get His full praise for it. " Ade was getting passionate Fela could tell by his tone of voice and the way it had increased in volume.

"Fela I haven't told anyone this but I'm looking

to set up an arts academy, where the youth can come and express themselves through music, dance, drama, sports, arts & crafts and a discussion forum. After all it is a person's talents that should be rewarded, they're God's special stamp of individuality on us all. Everyone has a great gift to offer humanity, each of us has a missing piece to the puzzle of life. These things need to be discovered and brought forward. Right now the only thing that gets society's praise is that whole celebrity culture which is based on shallow indulgences and vein ambition. According to the world, your important one-minute and then your not, it depends on the social climate. We need to show this world that in God's eyes your always important." Fela was truly impressed, he had heard his cousin speak before but this was a next level of reasoning he was expounding. Fela actually felt his head throbbing, it was like the size of Ade's words were too big for his mind to contain.

"So how are you gonna fund this academy?" Inquired Fela.

"I'll use some of my money as well as applying for sponsorship from the church, local businesses and government."

"Well bro I'm here to help you with whatever, just let me know what you want me to do."

"Yeah thanks cuzz, here take this." Ade reached into his bag and pulled out a folder with some sheets of paper in it and handed the folder to Fela. "This is a copy of the proposal for my project I've written up. Have a read of it and tell me what you think."

Fela took the folder and agreed to have a good read of it.

"Fela what you need you to do right now." Continued Ade. "Is you need to trust the power God has, to take you through the valley of the shadow of death. Never allow yourself to become subject to your circumstances, make them subject to you. Our wills are the gardens in which we plant our destines bro!" With that he bent over and potted one of his balls, it would have been a great shot if it was his go!

+   +   +

Since Shine's proposition a lot had been happening in the world of Calvin. Not only had he taken up the position of Shine's worker, he had also moved in with him. After he had the altercation with his sister he decided it would be best if he moved out. That day he told Shine about his situation and he agreed to let Calvin stay in his flat provided he continued to work for him. He went home the next day when his sister was out packed his stuff and left. That evening he phoned his sister telling her that he had moved out. They got into a vicious argument, which ended in Calvin, putting the phone down on her. Two days had passed since then and they still hadn't spoken.

Calvin was doing his best to blot it out of his memory. He was seeing more money than he had ever laid eyes on and he was earning respect from being seen with Shine.

"Calvin, buzz me up it's Roach." Said a high pitched

voice through the intercom. Calvin felt esteemed that someone like Carl Roach would call him by his name, he felt important because of it. There was a knock on the door a few minutes later and Calvin opened it. Roach stood there with a zoot (spliff) in his mouth, he touched fists with Calvin and stepped into the flat. Calvin couldn't help staring in adulation at the way Roach dressed. From head to toe he was decked out in designer apparel, and the diamond necklace and matching bracelet made him look all the more ghetto fabulous. Roach smiled as if he picked up on Calvin's admiration, he winked then walked over to the room where Shine was waiting for him. Calvin looked around at Shine's flat. To him this was what living was about, being filthy rich. It was to him the perfect picture of the gangster's paradise; leather chairs, big screen T.Vs amongst other, expensive commodities.

"Come we go." Shine's husky voice startled him, making him spin round. Shine was dressed in an expensive denim suit and sunglasses. The plan was for them to go and invest in a large consignment of narcotics. Calvin felt a rush of excitement, they were gonna roll in Shine's convertible, he couldn't wait to be seen with them.

On the way to their pick up point Shine decided he needed to take a detour. They turned into a local block of flats, Drayton Park Estate, it looked like most other inner city estates; a group of tower blocks that scraped the skyline. Shine got out in front of one block and beckoned Calvin to follow him, Roach was to stay in the car and watch for clampers. Shine led Calvin into a block of flats, explaining that he wanted to introduce one of his old friends to him. They walked down a dank corridor, where all the lights seemed to flicker. They stopped when they came to a red door, which had some paint chipped off.

"Paul open up I know you're in there." Shine shouted banging on the door. His tone wasn't fierce, it was unemotional almost placid but it still sounded threatening. When there was no answer he started to bang harder, swearing in between insults and threats to kick the door down. Calvin started to think there was no one in when he heard the sound of a baby crying. Shine began to bang even harder but still he didn't loose his cool. When no one came he started kicking the door. Almost immediately Calvin heard the sound of a door being unbolted.

"I'm coming, I'm coming." Came the sound of a voice Calvin guessed was Paul's. When the door opened there stood a man in front of them, he looked like he hadn't slept or washed in days.

"Sorry I was sleeping, I didn't hear." he murmured avoiding Shine's glare.

"Yeah whatever," Shine pushed him out of the way and marched into his house. Calvin reluctantly followed, the smell was repulsive and the flat looked dirty and messy. "Oi Paul I beg you shut that baby up, she's hotting me up, the neighbours might think something's going on." Paul left them in the corridor and disappeared into a room. "And while you're in there get my money." Shine shouted after him.

Calvin heard Paul's voice and another which

sounded like a woman's, they were arguing and trying to calm the baby down at the same time. Calvin's heart sunk when he heard what they were saying, "I had to spend the money the baby was hungry, plus the rent was due." "But you knew that money was for Shine." Shine just stood there looking defiant. He went over to the door and called Paul out.

"Look Shine can I give you the money tomorrow," He closed the door behind him softly, the baby had stopped crying. " I'll definitely have it for you then. My baby mother spent the money on food for our daughter and the rent, I never knew nothing about it, I swear." There was a moment's silence then out of nowhere Shine sparked Paul and sent him flying into the wall. Calvin's body jumped like he had just been hit, he swallowed hard trying to keep his horror hidden behind his silence.

"You're trying to take me for an idiot in it." Shouted Shine. Calvin saw a different level of wickedness in Shines eyes. It was like he was possessed by a demon, he started shouting profanity uncontrollably and he was kicking and punching. The baby was crying again by now and Paul's baby mother came running out to try to stop Shine. She grabbed him but Shine punched her and pushed her to the ground. Paul got up and was pleading with Shine.

"Look how long I've known you Shine, we grew up together blood, spare me, come on." Calvin started to do some pleading of his own but he tried his best to disguise his horror.

"Shine we need to bounce it's getting too hot, the

feds will be here any minute now, the neighbours have most probably called them because of all the noise." Shine stopped, his chest heaved up and down.

"You know what, I'm coming back at midnight I want my money tonight." Paul whimpered that he would have the money by midnight. Shine spat on the floor repeated his threat then left, followed by a very shaken up Calvin.

✦   ✦   ✦

Ade dropped Fela off at his house after the game of pool. Fela's mind was reeling with ideas. He had agreed with Ade that when the arts academy started he would assist in running a creative writing workshop. While he was in jail he used to attend one, so he had an idea of how to run one. Ade hinted at the fact that he would like to make an album, some music videos and a drama presentation with the youth. Fela thought that maybe it was his chance to make it big, if the project became a high profile initiative like Ade was planning. Fela's circle of influence would increase and he would have a platform on which he could launch his writing career. His mind was racing the rest of the night. He explained the idea to his mother and she told him to go for it but to find a job in the meantime to fund himself.

"It would be good for you to gain some experience in youth work before hand. Why don't you take that woman up on her offer." She was referring to Brenda's offer of voluntary work down at the youth club.

"I might do that but I need paid work as well. I

might just do another warehouse job in the meantime. I'm ready to do anything to make some funds, I've learnt now that sacrifice is the price tag on success."

"I'm glad to hear you talk like that my son, you will go far with that kind of thinking. Ever since you were young I've tried to drum in your head the fact that all the great people start at the bottom and make their way to the top. It's their ability to make the transition from top to bottom that makes them great. You've got to start somewhere even if it's in a job you hate. Just remember not to work for the money let the money work for you." Fela gave his mother a hug and a kiss and reminded her about their date on Friday to celebrate her birthday.

He went to his room with a lot on his mind, he sat contemplating what Ade had said about setting goals that were geared towards spreading God's love and using personal talents to achieve them. He knew he wanted to make it with his writing he just had to believe that he could do it.

The night was still young but he was tired. The night before he did not get much sleep because he had a lot on his mind. His lack of sleep was now catching up with him and he began to feel drowsy. He turned on the T.V and to his surprise he was on it. He was on stage performing a poem and everyone was shouting his name. He strained his ears but he could not quite catch the words. When he had finished the people began rushing the stage and grabbing him whilst still calling out his name. When he came to his senses, he realised it was his mum calling him and shaking him.

As his eyes came into focus he saw anxiety in her face.

"Mum what's wrong?" He sat up and held her by the shoulders. She wiped her teary eyes.

"I just received a call from the hospital, it's Ade he's been in a car accident, he's in a critical condition." Fela's heart skipped a beat like a scratched record then started beating fast like a sample that's been sped up. He got out of bed, put on his shoes and ordered a cab. It was midnight and he questioned whether he was really awake. He had left Ade in high spirits how could this be happening. *I know he's gonna be alright though,* he thought to himself, *what am I getting upset about?*

As they climbed into the cab he looked at his mother and he could see fear in her eyes.

"He'll be fine mum." He put his hand on hers and said a silent prayer. Neon lights whizzed by and late night revellers were pulled past his window in a flash. Everything was a blur, he felt tears creep into his eyes.

When they arrived at the hospital they were told to sit and wait for a doctor Khan. He arrived dressed in green overalls with a stressed expression on his face. He introduced himself and shook hands with Fela and his mum. He had the look of typical doctor, that of emotional detachment. It wasn't clear what he was feeling or what he would say. This made it hard for Fela to tell what he was about to hear, he just hoped for the best.

"So how is he?" Fela's mum cut to the chase. She was

at the edge of her seat and she looked worried. There was a tense silence, which made Fela feel uneasy.

"I'm sorry to inform you of this," the doctor started, he spoke calmly and slowly. Fela felt a lump in his throat; his mother's eyes were teeming with tears. "We tried everything we could do but we couldn't keep him… Ade passed away. There was a haemorrhage in his brain and he had lost a lot of blood." By this time Fela's mum was bawling uncontrollably, Fela had to hold her up, he could barely hold himself up, his knees felt weak. Everything felt surreal; he was just with him a few hours ago how could he be dead? His mind couldn't get round the reality and trying to do so made him feel dizzy.

The doctor called some nurses to come and comfort them. They were led to identify Ade's body. When Fela saw him it was his turn to brake down, to see his cousin lifeless, his face was scarred and disfigured. The sight made his stomach churn. He felt his mother's embrace as he fell to his knees. Everything around him was dark. It was like the sun had fallen from the sky and landed on his heart. He could feel the weight and the burning.

There was one question that echoed in his mind: *God why?*

8

"Dearly, beloved we are gathered here today, to remember our dear brother Ade." Pastor Blake's voice sounded solemn, he adjusted some papers on his pulpit and looked up, paused for a second then continued. He spoke about the tragedy of Ade's death and how it was a terrible loss and shock for everyone that knew him. Amongst the sombre faces, was Fela's, he stood next to his mother and also his aunt and uncle; Ade's, mum and dad. Sola, Ade's older sister, was also present, she had flown all the way from the States to be there. As the Pastor spoke Fela looked around at the crowd, he saw sad faces; many people were weeping including his mother and Ade's mother. Tears raced down his cheek as he stared in disbelief at Ade's picture on the stage. The last two weeks had been like a dream, he just couldn't believe what was happening, his thoughts were scattered like fragmented pieces of a shattered light bulb. Everything around him seemed dark. There was a pain in his chest, it felt like someone had taken his heart and crushed it.

He listened to the Pastor's words searching for an answer as to why God had taken such an inspirational figure from him. The world needed more people like that not less.

"I live by the saying expect the unexpected because life is full of uncertainties, you never know what will happen next." The Pastor paused to dab his eyes with his hanky. "If there is one thing you can be sure of, it is that we all have a common destiny in death. As harsh as it sounds it's a reality that we all have to face up to, sooner or later. Ecclesiastes expresses this point eloquently in chapter 3 verses 1-2, 'To every thing there is a season, and a time to every purpose under the heaven: A time to be born, and a time to die; a time to plant, and a time to pluck up that which is planted.' Some die young others die when they're old but you can rest assured that it will happen."

"Now this doesn't mean you have to live your life in constant fear of death because death for the Christian is not the end, it's the beginning of eternity. This experience we call life is only a means to an end, it is not the end in it's self. That's why even though one's passing may be a temporary loss for us, we should still find the strength to celebrate their life because, it is an eternal gain for heaven." There were shouts of 'Amen' from the crowd. Pastor Blake paused and looked into the crowd, Fela felt like the he was looking right at him and speaking directly to him. Fela was taking in everything the Pastor was saying but he hadn't had time to digest it all. He had been to funerals in the past but he had never paid attention to the preaching, he was running from God back then. All that he was hearing now was new to him.

The Pastor continued speaking for another five minutes or so then he started calling for those who had speeches to come up. Fela felt his heart sink, when he heard the Pastor call for him to come up. He knew that he was gonna make a speech at some point but he didn't feel ready. His legs seemed to have a mind of their own because they were leading him to the stage against his wishes.

"I just wanna say thank you to everyone for coming." Fela's voice trembled with emotion He looked down at his papers, his eyes were blurry with tears. He took in a deep breath, bit his bottom lip and looked up, he had to be strong it's what Ade would have wanted. "These last two weeks have been extremely difficult and my family and I appreciate all the love and support you have all given." Fela paused to compose himself. "About my cousin, well he was a real solider. From fighting to protect me when I was younger to fighting to get me out of jail and see me change, he was always fighting for me." The crowd bubbled with a little laughter at his statement, which eased his tension, allowing him to grin a little. He told them about how when he got locked up Ade never judged him but instead he gave him words of encouragement and prayed for him. It was Ade's tenacious faith that inspired Fela to start having a relationship with God again.

"I'm not gonna stand here and lie saying 'Ade was perfect and he never had any faults.' No, just like everyone Ade made mistakes but he learnt from them and tried never to repeat them again. He wasn't only a cousin to me he was a true friend who could always brighten up my day. He showed me that you don't have to go to Hollywood to find stars. His strong faith was a constant source of inspiration to me and because he kept it up to the end I see it as a personal victory for him. I once heard someone say that clapping was the sound of victory and I would like it very much if you would give my cousin a round of applause." The crowd obliged him with a thunderous clapping that seemed to inspire a sense of triumph in Fela. He walked off the stage feeling stronger.

After the service there was a short party to celebrate Ade's life. There was not going to be a trip to the cemetery because Ade's body was being shipped to Nigeria, he was going to be buried there. There was a park across the road from the church and Fela decided to seek refuge there for a while, he wanted to escape the crowded church and get some peace and quiet. It was a beautiful day, the sun was shining and the birds were singing. He sat on a bench trying to make sense of everything going on around him. Something pricked his bottom as he sat down, he jumped up abruptly looking around at the bench. There was a rose on the bench, he had sat on it without noticing it. *Life's a joke that ain't funny*, he thought to himself, picking up the pink rose, *how can something so beautiful bring such pain.* He wasn't just thinking of the rose he meant life as well. It was a beautiful day but yet it carried with it something so hurtful. He saw the rose as an analogy for life. *To live is the flower to die is the thorn.* The thought made his eye swell with tears.

"Fela." He wiped his eyes, then turned round to see the golden brown face of Sapphire, looking straight back at him. She looked concerned as if she knew how distressed he was.

"I hope I didn't frighten you?" She said, cracking an awkward smile. Fela shook his head, trying to smile back at her.

"Nah, Nah it's cool. Where you off to?"

"I've got to go home, there's a pile of Uni work I need to finish for tomorrow, sorry. Fela told her she didn't need to apologise, her coming to show her support was enough for him. She smiled in reply to Fela's modesty. It was a cheerful smile that made Fela feel warm inside. Sapphire was about to take her leave from him when she stopped and looked him dead in the eye saying:

"I know you've most probably heard this a hundred times today but I feel the need to echo it. I just want to tell you that your cousin Ade was a great man and he'll be truly missed by all of us. You've got to trust God to help you make sense of it all." Fela dropped his gaze from hers and let out a mock laugh.

"I hope He can 'cause right now I'm confused. Ade was a soldier we needed right now." Fela paused trying to find the words that would express his true sentiment. "He had so much to offer the community. Why would God take someone like that, those are the people we need more of, it's the wicked people that need to go." He kissed his teeth in frustration.

"Do you know it was a drug addict who made him crash." Continued Fela. Sapphire replied that she had heard something but didn't know the full story. She sat down on the bench to listen to him. He explained how the junkie was in the middle of a robbery and he ran out in front of Ade's car. Ade swerved to avoid hitting him and ended up skidding and crashing into a lamppost. The junkie made a break for it but the police caught up with him eventually, because he had been mindless enough to leave them one vital clue, his bus pass.

"He may be locked up now but at least he's still alive. It seems like bad things always happen to good people. How ironic is that, I'm telling you life is a joke that ain't funny." Fela sighed and put his hand over his eyes.

"I hear what you're saying," Sapphire started. "It's a shame that such an inspirational figure was taken from us at a time when he was most needed. Why God would take him away at this time, I do not know. What I do know is that Ade may not be with us physically but his soul lives on through his legacy. He was and still is an inspirational character and it is down to us to continue the work he started. We may have lost Ade but we still have God and our lives to make a positive change in this world. We will see Ade again and we owe it to him to have a positive legacy to give like the one he gave us." Fela got up as she finished speaking.

"I'd better be heading back. I appreciate everything you're saying it's definitely something I'll think about."

He shook hands with her and as she was walking she shouted over her shoulder:

"Remember to pray, God does listen. If you need anything don't hesitate to call me." Fela thanked her and went on his way. He was feeling slightly uplifted but there was still a heavy weight on his heart.

9

A week had gone by since the funeral but to Fela it felt like an eternity. Each day he had stayed locked away in his room, a prisoner to misery. He hadn't shaved in weeks, his room was in a mess and he had stopped writing.

"Fela," His mother sounded like the police the way she knocked on his door. "There's someone on the phone for you."

"Well tell them I'm sleeping." He called out from under his covers. He then heard his mum apologising to Sapphire on his behalf. Then there was a knock at the door again.

"Come in." His mother entered the room.

"Fela look at the state of this place!" she shrieked, opening the curtain and the window. "How long are you gonna keep this up?"

"What?" Fela asked, pretending he didn't know what she meant.

"You know what, shutting yourself away like this is unhealthy, it's not good for the mind, the body or the spirit. You know they say the state of a person's room reflects the state of their mind, just take a look at yours." He looked around his room. There were unwashed plates on the windowsill, clothes (dirty and clean) were scattered all over the place along with shoes and papers.

"Yeah well right now I can't face life, I feel disorientated and tired. This is all just too much for me to bare right now." Fela replied, still under the covers.

"It's a lot for all of us to bare on our own, that's why we've got each other, so we can strengthen one another. Staying in here and bottling everything up isn't helping, it's just making things worse." His mother sat by the edge of the bed. "There are so many people around you that are willing to lend their support to you. It's just a matter of you taking it. You need to let go and let God." Her words were like honey to his bitter heart. The weight he felt was not so much Ade's death, it was more the anger he felt towards the guy that caused the accident. Inside of him was an insatiable desire for revenge, he wanted to pay the junkie back for what he did, but his mother's words made him reconsider. He just had to let it go, otherwise his anger would consume him, he needed to let God deal with the matter; only He had the power and wisdom to. As he got up to face his mother he found himself wiping tears from his eyes. His mother hugged him and he felt a slight moment of *déjà vu*. He was reminded of the day when his dad left and he was crying, it was the same scene, someone he needed had left him and his mother was there for him.

It was late afternoon and after speaking with his mum Fela decided to go to the barbers to get a trim. Ramona worked there and he wanted to see her, he wanted to explain why he had been avoiding her calls. He entered the barbers and was immediately hit by the beautiful voice of a young girl who was singing, *"His eye is on the sparrow."* Everyone was stood around the young lady as she serenaded their ears with rich harmonies. Fela, who recognised the girl as Ramona's younger cousin Kizzy, was totally blown away. He stood by the door till she finished then he approached her, whilst she was being showered with clapping and shouts for an encore.

"What's up Kizzy?" Fela hugged her and applauded her singing. She was a young girl around fifteen with a pretty face and a friendly smile, Fela looked on her like a little sister. "Where's Ramona?"

"She went to go and collect Kenya from the child minders," Kizzy replied. "She'll be back in a short while."

One of the barbers requested that Kizzy should sing a love ballad. She obliged them and went straight into a performance.

A barber Fela had never seen before called him over. The man was tall with dark skin and cornrows. He had a heavy West Indian accent and he mumbled which made it hard for Fela to comprehend what he was saying. Fela asked him where B was, that was his usual barber. The guy muttered something about a holiday, so Fela figured B was obviously away. The man offered to trim him but at first Fela thought he was saying "do you want him", in reference to B and there was a misunderstanding until another barber translated what he was saying as "do you wan trim". Fela contemplated the cut he did for the guy who was getting out of his chair. It looked all right so he agreed to let the man trim him.

He got in the chair and looked in the mirror. He hadn't looked this rough since he first came out of jail, he had grown a beard all around and his hair looked bushy and unkempt. His eyes had a strained look, like all the life and brightness was being sucked out of them.

"How do you want it?" The man's voice was deep.

"Keep my beard, but take it down and give me a number 1 on my head." The man grunted a response, which made Fela uneasy, but he just couldn't be bothered to say anything. The man began to trim him and all was going well on top. Then he came to the beard and the man just completely flipped the script. He started scrapping away at the beard like there was no tomorrow. Fela wanted cuss him but he left it till after. When the man was finished, Fela surveyed the damage; his beard was gone, he just had a thin moustache and some thin sideburns. The only thing that he was ok with was the level of his hair.

"I told you to leave the beard man!" His tone was quite aggressive. The barber muttered an apology and claimed he never heard that part. Fela was mad but he decided to let it go and just give the man his six pound fee . As he was getting up, Ramona entered the shop with Kenya, as soon as he saw them Fela forgot his vexation and ran over to them.

"Kenya! Hi missy, how are you?" He picked Kenya up and gave her a kiss on the cheek. He then hugged Ramona and explained to her what had happened with the barber. She told him that Tyrell, the barber was new, and to forget it because the trim looked "cool".

"How's it going. How are you holding up?" She asked him.

"I'm doing ok. I still can't believe that Ade's gone, it just hasn't sunk in yet." An expression of sadness formed on Fela's face, he sighed heavily.

"I know what you're saying," said Ramona. "When I lost my mum, nothing made sense anymore. I didn't know how me and Calvin were going to cope." She paused to reminisce.

"How's Calvin?" Fela wanted to change the subject to one more desirable but that was all he could think of, he had never been any good at breaking awkward silences .

"I couldn't tell you," Ramona let out a sigh and put Kenya into a chair. "I haven't seen or heard from him all week. He doesn't stay with me, and he doesn't answer my calls either. He says he's staying with a friend but I don't know where."

"Give me his number I'll try and talk some sense into him." Fela offered.

"Nah, you don't know Calvin, he finds it hard to listen to the voice of reason.

He's one of those hard-headed kids, he won't learn till he feels it. I just pray nothing drastic happens to him that's all." She let out an awkward laugh. "Besides you've got enough problems to deal with. I think you're very brave, the speech you gave at the funeral really moved me, I didn't know Ade that well but from what I knew he was a decent man just like you are." At that moment a young fine woman came through the door. She gave Fela a smile and then turned to Ramona.

"Good afternoon Mrs Campbell, just take a seat, I'll be with you in a minute." Mrs Campbell greeted her and sat down in Ramona's chair. "Fela I need to go I've got an appointment but bell me so we can link up." Fela said he would then after saying good bye to her and Kenya he went on his way, his next stop was the book shop.

He entered the shop to find Decent arranging books on the shelf. When Decent turned and saw Fela coming through the door he looked astonished.

"Hello Fela." Decent turned to greet him, explaining that he had been trying to contact him, but only ever got Fela's voicemail. Fela explained that he had kept his phone off because of the whole Ade situation, which Decent knew nothing of.

"I did get your message and everything but I just wasn't in the mood to speak to anybody, it was nothing personal, it's just how I felt at the time." Decent expressed his deepest sympathies regarding the death of Ade, saying he understood Fela's need to be alone.

"Nah, it's cool these things happen, you've just got to get on with it. You can't wallow in misery forever." Fela tried his best to sound positive. "Anyway what was it you wanted to talk about." Decent had left a message on his phone saying he wanted to talk to him about a pressing issue.

"Well I have a job proposition for you if you're interested." Fela implied he was by a nod of his head. "Well it's just that in a few weeks time I'm going to start doing some story telling in a number of primary schools and I need someone to fill in for me here, are you interested." Fela affirmed that he was "on it" and he would be ready to start whenever.

"Well if your not doing anything now, you could start today if you want." Fela agreed and phoned his mum to tell her the good news. Decent spent the rest of the afternoon showing Fela how to serve customers, fill shelves and to fill the account books.

"All of this sounds confusing." Fela exclaimed, his head felt like a washing machine set on spin dry.

"Ah don't worry about it young sir, it's like driving a car, it's confusing the first time but as you get used to it, it becomes second nature. You'll be fine, trust me, besides it's only for a few hours in the morning." Fela felt a bit reassured and as Decent showed him the ropes he became more confident.

The afternoon went by quite fast, there were a few customers that came in and out but most of the time Fela spent reasoning with Decent.

"You shouldn't refer to yourself as black." said Decent, in the middle of Fela's discourse on "the plight of the black man". "If you look at it the word black has many negative connotations attached to it. When we think of black we think of evil, death, grime, dirt, darkness. How can we use a word that has these negative images attached to it, to describe who we are?"

"So what should we call ourselves then?" Fela cracked a cheeky smile.

"Nubians, that's what we are. The name sounds more pleasant and has attached to it the legacy of Kings and Queens who achieved phenomenal feats and were, according to historians, the "Fathers of civilisation". Decent pointed to a few books as he spoke.

"But can you really say that calling ourselves Nubians will bring about a significant change in the way we perceive ourselves. Look at all our forefathers who went before us, they were called all kinds of names under the sun but that made them more determined to achieve." Fela believed that the truth should stand under serious scrutiny so he questioned everything as far as he could. He felt what Decent was saying but he needed to be sure it was a solid argument.

"I'm not saying that it's going to wash away all of our problems but I believe it's a step in the right direction. Yeah there were Nubian leaders who called themselves black and were still positive but what they fought so hard to change hasn't really changed. The negative self-image is still there, Nubian's now call themselves Niggers, as a term of endearment. They give each other dirty looks on the high street, they call their women bitches. There is a serious problem here. In order to deal with this issue we need to get to the root of it, but how can we when we've lost connection with our roots. The word Nubian gives us that connection, it's a solid foundation to build on. Rally's, fighting, speeches they're all just social aspirin, their effects don't last. There needs to be a change on the inside, a paradigm shift, which is only possible when we change how we view ourselves. Either consciously or sub-consciously, the word "Black" has connotations that effect how we view ourselves."

Fela didn't know what to say, he could see the logical sense in the argument, but the problem he saw was how to convince everyone else.

"Don't worry about convincing everyone else, just make the change in yourself first." Decent said after Fela had expressed his doubts. "Once people see the confidence and the success that comes from your paradigm shift, they will naturally follow."

Fela noticed that Decent had a Bible open by his counter.

"I didn't know you were a Christian, Decent."

"I'm not." Decent replied. Fela felt a sudden feeling of dismay.

"Oh."

"Yeah, I'm just interested in religion. I think there is a lot to learn from them. I've read the Bible, the Koran, as well as a bit of the Bhagavad-Gita." As he spoke, Decent opened a draw, which contained the books he spoke of. He explained to Fela that he was on a quest for the truth and he wanted to do extensive research before he committed himself to any belief.

"I've seen bits of truth in each of these books," he said gesturing at the books as he spoke. "I'm not saying that all religions are true because that would be me condoning any and every belief system. I believe the most truthful religions are those that teach equality, peace, respect and charity, both in word and deed." Fela listened with keen interest; he had had these debates with people before so he already had an idea of how to answer Decent.

"I was brought up in a Christian home and my wife was a Christian," Decent continued. "So I know a lot about Christianity, and I admire the teachings but where is the proof that it's the ultimate truth?"

"I have proof but it's of a personal nature. When I was 14, I got caught in the mist of robbing a betting shop, with some older boys. I was facing a lengthy sentence and everyone was praying for me at my mum's church. I was scared so I prayed; I told God if he let me off I would never do it again. Then my cousin came to me saying he had heard from God that I would be released. A couple days later I went to court and I was given a suspended sentence."

"What happened to the other boys?" Inquired Decent, he squinted his eyes. "They all got birded off, 6 years each. Another boy who was part of a separate case got a prison sentence for street robbery and it was his first offence so you know God had mercy on me."

"So why is it that you went to jail in the end then?"

"Well that was because I broke my promise, three years later I thought I would try my hand at fraud. I knew someone who was working for Royal Mail as a postman and my bredrin, offered me the deal of a lifetime; 5 g's if I got him five credit cards. To cut a long story short I took the bait and I got caught. They reeled us both in and we got sentenced to 6 years each.

I did four and now I'm out but my friend's still in there because he had an assault charge as well, he'll be out in a year." Decent looked pensive.

"So you're saying that it was the God of the Bible that answered your prayers?" Fela nodded.

"I've only ever known one God and that's who I pray to and that's who guides me." Fela explained. "All I can do is tell other people of what He has done for me and I believe that He will validate it as the truth."

With all their talking and the reasoning the time to close crept on them like a thief in the night.

"So what did you think of your first day?" Asked Decent as he closed the shutters.

"It was cool, I know that it's usually more busy than it was today but I reckon I can handle it." Decent assured him that he'd be all right.

"So what are you up to tonight?" Inquired Decent.

"Nothing much." Replied Fela.

"Well do you want to follow me down to "Express yourself" that's the Forum that Scott helps to run along with some of his friends." Fela had forgotten who Scott was so Decent reminded him, that he was the Caucasian guy who came to buy books the last time Fela was in the Shop. Fela found it hard to recall the incident, he had a very bad memory, he put it down to the amount of weed he used to smoke.

"Yeah I'll come down with you, why not." He made sure he phoned his mum, after the incident with Ade, she got scared when Fela stayed out late without telling her.

The Forum was being held at the local community

centre. The debate had already started by the time they arrived so they entered and quietly took a seat. Fela looked around the room, the chairs were set out in a circle and most of them were full. They were occupied mostly by black people but there were members from other ethnic groups present. Fela was a bit stunned to see Brenda, Calvin's youth worker sitting opposite him. She was seated next to a young Caucasian man who Fela recognised was the Scott that Decent was speaking of.

The debate was focused on education and why it was failing the youth, especially the Afro-Caribbean youth. Fela decided to keep quiet and listen to what was being said. The debate was intense and it got so heated at one point that a young man had to be asked to leave. Fela took note of a lot of the good points that were raised including: stronger teacher and parent relationships, parent support from the wider community, a more culturally sensitive curriculum and more ethnic minority school governors.

The talk lasted just over an hour and a half and when it finished Fela went over to talk to Brenda.

"What a pleasant surprise to see you here." She said extending her arm for him to shake. Fela explained that he had come with Decent, who he found Brenda happened to already be aquatinted with. She said she wanted to introduce Fela to someone and called Scott over. He was introduced as her husband but she was surprised to find out that they had already met.

"We keep bumping into each other Fela," Brenda

exclaimed, "I think it's Fate saying we've got to do some work together."

"Yeah," rejoined Scott, "it's either that or Fela might be stalking us!" They all enjoyed a brief moment of laughter.

"What's so funny?" Decent was standing next to Fela grinning.

"Nah we were just saying how much of a small world it was." Fela broke down the situation to Decent.

"You should have worked it out before, I told you his wife worked at the BIG Thinking project."

"Yeah but I forgot that's what the youth club's called now. Back in the day it was the No.8 club." Laughed Fela. Scott explained that the name was changed because they saw it as a new beginning and they wanted to reinvent the club's image.

They bantered for a while till Fela felt it was time to leave. He was tired and Decent needed him at the shop early the next day. Before he went to sleep he analysed his day. Things had turned around for him dramatically, he was starting to feel inspired by life again.

10

"How did you find the forum yesterday?" Decent asked, the next morning at work.

"It was cool, the problem was that I felt like there were too many ego's in the room." replied Fela. "At one point it looked like there was gonna be a fight, between two of the brothers in there."

"Yeah you do get that in those kind of arenas, especially when men are in front of women, we loose our heads to some macho guillotine. That's why I say we should try to reason more instead of always debating and arguing. At least with reasoning you are trying find a common ground with the next person."

"Don't you think it's true that one man's passion can be misconstrued by the next man as arrogance or aggression." Asked Fela with a perplexed look on his face.

"This is it," replied Decent clapping his hands. "There is a thin line between the two, trust me I know from experience. One just has to make sure they are not forcing their opinion on anyone. Even if you can't see eye to eye, at least try to keep your eyes, instead of making each other blind. A little strife, a little discord can eventually break out into a full-scale war." Decent let out a short laugh.

"Yeah, I know exactly what you're talking about." Laughed Fela. "There have been times when I've been so headstrong, I've refused to listen to the other person's view."

"We all do it and do you know why?" Decent's gold tooth sparkled as spoke.

"It's because we lack humility. A man can have all the knowledge in the world, but without humility that knowledge is as useful as a spade without an arm to use it."

"You've got some deep words Decent, you really know how to speak to a man's heart." Fela looked touched by the conversation they were having. After a brief interruption from a customer they resumed.

"You spoke of me being deep," Decent laughed. "You try working in a bookshop for 18 years and see what it does to your mind. You'll find your mind open so wide a freight train could fit through it. " They both laughed.

"You know Brenda wants me to do some voluntary work down at the youth club." Fela said, after he had finished serving a customer.

"Are you going to do it?" Decent was at a shelf with a pen and pad in his hand.

"I don't know, right now I don't think I can afford to work for free."

"You're not working for free, see it as an investment.

The rich experience you'll have in the long run will be of major benefit to you. Plus isn't the Christian message all about charity."

"Yeah," said Fela admittedly. "I guess it is."

"The example set by the apostles was one of charity and love." Decent chewed on his pen as he spoke. He was still looking at the shelves, he told Fela he was doing a stock count. "The Disciples never owned property, they sold everything and shared it amongst themselves, the only currency they had was love. Communities could learn a lot from them about co-operation, especially when it comes to money. It's a concept borrowed by socialists and the African principle of Ujima has similar connotations."

"I've heard of Ujima, what does it mean again?"

"It is the concept of true unity." Decent interlocked his fingers to demonstrate his point. "It states that each has a responsibility for themselves as well as a responsibility to care for other members of the community."

"What like 'Love thy neighbour as thy self'?"

"Exactly," said Decent clapping his hands and giving Fela the thumbs up. "That means that if there is a problem in the community we need to put our minds together to resolve it. This can only be done through co-operation and a caring attitude. In the words of the poet John Donne, 'no man is an Island' we are our brother's keepers as well as our sister's."

"Everyone's out for themselves these days, it's all about outshining everyone else. That's why we have this celebrity, bling culture, it's the untamed ego at work. Only a humble man or woman, would share their riches with one who is worse off than them." Decent went into the back to get a book for a customer while Fela took an order over the phone.

"Man, it's so hard to be humble when everywhere you turn society is trying to charm your vanity," complained Fela. "You're bombarded with messages and images that appeal to your ego on a daily basis."

"It's true the media does prey on human weaknesses." Decent laughed. "They know that humans are inherently insecure, so they sell them the dreams they want.

This celebrity culture is that dream, everybody wants to feel wanted and noticed, fame and fortune offer this in the form of security and a sense of belonging."

"These psychologists know it and the media has picked up on it, that's why they exploit our weaknesses. Sex is one of them." At this point Decent picked up a news paper. There was a story on the front page about the rise in teenage pregnancies and how it was becoming an epidemic. Then Decent turned a few pages and there was a picture of a glamour model exposing her breasts.

"They complain about the teenage pregnancy rate on one page but on the next they are promoting lustful thinking." Fela was shocked by what he was seeing. He was a man who was finding it hard to practise celibacy as a Christian, and seeing things like that made him feel like there was no hope.

"They complain that there are too many kids

having sex under the age of 16 yet walk into your local sweet shop, sex is everywhere. On the shelves the porn magazines are near the teenage magazines and near the sweets. The kids are obviously seeing it all, and it's going to have an effect on their vulnerable minds." Decent's way of speaking was captivating and Fela was hearing every word he was saying. He didn't mind letting Decent speak while he listened as long as he was learning something. Many people wouldn't be able to dig the deep convo's that he liked to have with people. He wasn't a man that liked to banter so whenever he spoke with people the conversation was weighty, what else was there to talk about that was worth his breath. He was a thinker and he felt free whenever he opened his mind to philosophise.

"It's the love of money that makes people prey on the weaknesses of others, that's why moral decay in our country is rife." Fela interjected. "It's deep because no one wants to face up to the reality, everyone's caught up in the mirage. It's up to people like us to go out and educate the masses."

"That's right, there needs to be a sense of Ujima in all of us." Proclaimed Decent, he spoke like he was decreeing a new law, in the House of Commons. "We need to come together in unity no matter what the cost. With the Civil rights boycott of the Bus system, many people made sacrifices to get the laws changed. Anything worth fighting for will require sacrifice."

Fela felt compelled to phone Brenda after he and Decent had finished their discourse. He asked Decent to use the phone.

"Yeah sure go ahead."

Fela picked up the phone and dialled Brenda's number.

"Hello."

"Hello, may I speak to Brenda please?"

"Speaking." Came the reply. Fela made his identity known then explained to Brenda that he would like to do some voluntary work after all.

"So what made you change your mind?" Asked Brenda.

"Well let's just say that love is stronger than pride. I've realised that if I want to make a difference in society I've got to make some sacrifices, and if working without pay is one of them then so be it, I'll humble myself and do it. The way I see it is, that I'm making a long-term investment with a form of social capital: Love!"

As they were closing the shop that day Fela's phone rang, it was Sapphire, the Pastor's daughter. Fela apologised for not returning her calls. She had tried him quite a few times in the last week. She told him there was an open mic poetry jam going on and asked if he would like to go.

"Yeah, that should be cool, how are we getting down there?"

"I'm driving, I've got my Dad's car for the night."

They arranged to meet at the train station and Fela, phoned his mother to let her know his plans. The station was a short walk from the bookshop and he reached there within no time. Not too long after, Sapphire pulled up in her Dad's Range Rover jeep.

Fela's heart was racing, there was something about her presence that captivated him. When he first met her he knew that he liked her, but he didn't want to admit it to himself. He was trying to stay focused on defining his purpose before he got involved in a relationship. He didn't want anymore complications in his life and to him that's what relationships were. All the girls he had ever linked always seemed to hinder him from moving forward, until he was sure that every girl was trying to "work brain" on him. He was convinced that all females wanted to do was play mind games and that was something he didn't have time for. Ade used to tell him he was paranoid but he begged to differ, his experience was his evidence.

"It's like women beg for a good man to come along," he complained once to Ramona "but when that good man comes they're like 'he's too soft' or 'he's not confident enough'. They actually mistake your humility for weakness and start taking liberties with you." Ramona just replied with a giggle.

Fela had to admit though, Sapphire did seem genuine. There was something real about the way she looked. No fake nails, no make up, her hair was natural and she wore a necklace made from beads. Her brown eyes seemed soft and friendly, yet Fela still felt awkward around her. The day he first met her, at her fathers house he avoided her as much as he could, at first he thought it was nerves but when he thought about it, he realised it was deeper than that. It was like she seemed almost too good to be true, he felt if he pursued her in anyway he might be disappointed.

Plus he noticed the watchful eye of the Pastor on him every time he went near her and that definitely added to the feeling of awkwardness.

Sapphire was elaborately dressed in a denim jacket, a long skirt and boots. Fela had just flung on a tracksuit, he had not been in the mood to dress up, but after seeing Sapphire looking fly, he thought he should have made more of an effort.

They chatted away as they drove to the Bar where the event was going to be held. Sapphire told Fela she was studying law at university and how she hoped to go to law school when she finished. Fela told her he wanted to get into youth work and that he planned to one day release a book of poetry. As they talked Fela started to feel more comfortable around her, especially when he found out she was single.

"Thanks for the talk the other day, it really inspired me," said Fela over the sound of some jazz music. "I've decided that I'm going to carry on my cousins work. He had a dream of starting up an Arts Academy and I'm going make his dream a reality." Fela explained Ade's idea for an Academy to her. She said it was really positive and if he needed any help he should ask her.

"Are you going to perform for us tonight then?" She asked expectantly.

"I don't know I might, it depends on what the crowd's like. I don't want to tackle a difficult crowd, especially because I haven't performed in front of a crowd for a while."

They arrived at the bar just before the show started. The place was dimly lit with red lights and some candles. People from all walks of life were present and the atmosphere was very vibrant. Sapphire knew quite a few people in there, she had told Fela she attended these sort of events regularly. Fela was introduced to people most of whom he didn't get their names. It was impossible to hear over the music and the constant droning of people's conversation.

The show started and the different artists started performing. The acts consisted of mainly poets and singers but there were a few miscellaneous acts as well. Fela thought that most of the acts were good and he watched them for inspiration. Then the host announced that he had a few more spaces if anyone else wanted to step up to the mic and perform. Fela felt nervous but seeing as the crowd were not too bad and Sapphire kept telling him to do it; he went to put his name down.

Whilst he was waiting to perform he was alright but when the host called his name, he felt his heart sinking and his throat drying up, his legs felt like they would give way but he still approached the stage. He took the mic and introduced himself and the poem he was going to perform, which was entitled 'swollen eyes'. He was inspired to write it after witnessing the fight Ramona had with her brother Calvin. It was a poem about all the sadness and pain the human race is causing and how we are ignorant to it. At first his voice was shaky but by the time he got to the end of the first verse he started to feel more relaxed. He repeated the chorus, 'I've got swollen eyes but the only thing I've been fighting are my tears' and he heard Sapphire repeating it with him. After the second verse when he came to the chorus not only Sapphire, but most of the people in the place, were singing his song. The round of applause he got was electrifying and he left the stage grinning from ear to ear.

"That was amazing." Sapphire said to him as he rejoined her by the bar. "What do you want to drink? It's on me." Fela thanked her for the support and generosity she had shown him.

"I'll have an orange juice please," he said. "I've got to get to work early tomorrow and plus I'm already drunk off my own success, I wouldn't want to make it worse with alcohol." They both laughed as Sapphire ordered the drinks in.

11

Calvin carefully licked the edge of the rizzla paper and started gently rolling it up into a spliff.

"Man!" he protested as the rizzla paper ripped. Being a beginner he still hadn't mastered the art of "billin" (rolling up) yet and he had licked the rizzla sheet too much so it split. Since he had started smoking he had mostly been getting passes, but now he had decided he needed to be an independent blazer if he was going to get respect from the rest. Shine didn't really mind the fact that he started smoking, but of course he wasn't allowed to get high on Shine's supply.

"If I find out that you've been dipping your hands into my merchandise, I'll break both of them." was the modest warning Shine gave him, and as he liked having the use of both his hands, Calvin chose to obey.

"Here blood!" A shrewd looking brother who Calvin knew by the name B, passed a soggy spliff, with all but the butt left to smoke. Calvin turned it down, he didn't fancy smoking the roach and plus he was buzzing already, the fumes alone were enough to make him high. He laid back in Shine's leather chairs and observed the scenery. The flat was packed out with all types of shady characters, most of whom Calvin had never met before. There were some young girls from around Calvin's way, up in there; they were no older than Calvin was, around 14 or 15. They danced for Shine's guests, who were all in their mid 20's and above. Some disappeared with the girls only to return minutes later looking extremely pleased with themselves.

This is it, thought Calvin as he lounged on Shine's sofa, *I can actually say I've lived the thug life, what all the rappers talk about I'm living it.* He took a sip of some of the Baileys he had on the table, then spluttered it out in an involuntary spate of coughing. Some of the crowd turned to ask if he was ok, Calvin looking embarrassed replied he was fine then picked up a newspaper to see if there was anything interesting on T.V.

He didn't know if it happened because he was high, but he was sure that the words on the page leapt out at him. There on the front page it had a picture of Paul, the druggie with the headline:

"Kids find O.D Junkie dead in park."

He couldn't believe what he was reading; he had sold Paul something two nights before and he was found the morning after. All kinds of questions were swarming his mind. *Was I the one that sold him his last fix? Did I kill him? Does Shine know? Did Shine kill him for not paying him?* His weed filled mind was foggy and it was spinning like a windmill. Indigestion tossed and turned in his stomach like a sea in a storm. Sweat oozed onto his brow as he remembered Shine's words.

"When it comes to my money I don't play." Shine had once exclaimed, twisting his lips and spitting on the floor. "No body comes up short with me, not even a midget."

Paul hadn't paid Shine the exact money he owed him at the appointed time, he was £100 short of the £300 he owed. Shine told him to "forget it, it's cool" but when he was alone with Calvin he told him he only let Paul off because he would make him pay another way.

It was all too much for Calvin, he felt like he was going to be sick. He needed to talk to Shine but he was out, "attending to some business". No one in the room seemed to have even noticed his distress. They had the sound system on full blast and they were laughing and talking so loud, anyone would think they were competing to see who could make the most noise. He got up and crept out, he needed some fresh air, his belly felt like a tumble dryer and his head felt like someone had hit it with a sledge hammer.

The midnight air outside was cool. Calvin walked over to the lift; he needed to go for a walk. He pressed the button then remembered the lift was out of order so he decided to use the stairs. When he reached the top of the stairs his stomach convulsed. Regurgitated dona kebab and Baileys lay wasted on the floor at his feet, it was all he had eaten that day and his stomach felt totally emptied.

He had barely been able to compose himself when he heard the sound of footsteps on the stairs, accompanied by a familiar voice.

"...So you got him then? ...," It was Shine, his brassy voice echoed as he came up the stairway. He sounded a little distressed. "Ok...so when do I get my papers... but we had a deal, I deliver him to you and I'll get paid for it the next day...what complications?" Calvin heard him stop where he was. "What delay? There were at least 30 kilo's in Rico's yard as well as guns, what more do you want? You've got so much evidence on him you won't even need to throw the book at him, the book will throw itself. What are you waiting for? ..." Shine started to ascend the stairs again, then he stopped suddenly, his tone softened. "...Alright, alright I'm not trying to tell you what to do I'm just anxious that's all...well let me know alright?...bye." Calvin heard Shine's footsteps on the stairs so he moved up to next flight and waited till he had past. When he was sure Shine had gone into the yard he made his descent down the stairs but as he walked past his vomit, the very sight and smell of it made him queasy and he threw up again.

12

"…A North London Drug Baron was jailed for 18 years today. Rico Williams, aged 33, was given a maximum of 18 years in jail after police raided his home in Tulsbury, and found 25 kilos of cocaine and a large sum of cash. Police also found illegal firearms as well as some marijuana…"

Pastor Michael Blake and his wife, Vi were sat on their couch listening to the news report with sadness in their hearts.

"That's another lost soul locked up." Vi kissed her teeth and shook her head. "May God help us, how many more of these young men are going to loose their freedom before the rest realise that they're bumping their heads against a brick wall?"

"Only God knows Vi, only God knows." The Pastor rubbed his right hand down his face and sighed. "The youth these days are so caught up, that when you try and speak to them and show them another way, they don't have the scope to see it. They have one track minds and the only way forward for them is through illegal street life."

"There must be a way that we can reach them." Vi was trying her best to be optimistic.

"I believe there is Vi, but it's going to be a lot of work and right now nobody doesn't seem to want to volunteer. In a country run by sanctimonious politicians and occupied by a philistine majority, one finds it hard to see any hope for the future."

"Mike you mustn't give up hope," Vi turned to look her husband in the eye and held his hand. Her beauty had not faded in the 25 years they had been married. It had only matured, growing more and more bright like a rising sun. "Don't let the devil take away your hope, in a world of uncertainty hope is all you have. Hope is what keeps you going day to day even when things aren't going the way you planned. Just put your hope in God, He'll never fail you, for the Bible says that God is a solid rock. Build your hopes on God who can do what may seem impossible."

✦   ✦   ✦

It was the day of the gala and Fela was rolling up there with Sapphire and her cousin Warren. Sapphire was driving her mother's car; her dad had the jeep that day. Fela and Sapphire had become really tight over the last couple months since Ade's death; she had really been there to support him. He was developing feelings for her but he didn't want to rush into anything, before he gave his heart to a woman, he wanted to know that she was the right one.

"So what's it like over there?" Sapphire asked Fela, as they were driving. They had been discussing traditional foods and Fela had told them of his favourite Nigerian dishes.

"Where, Nigeria?" Fela replied, turning to make eye contact with Sapphire, she nodded. "I can't really remember it properly, I went when I was 6. I remember it being really hot and I remember the crowded market places but that's about it really.

Mind you from what I've heard there is a lot of corruption and poverty out there."

"You get that in most countries though." Replied Sapphire.

"Yes, but over there it is more blatant." Fela paused. "Don't get the wrong idea, Nigeria is not all bad. The culture is beautiful, the music, the food and the discipline is something special. My mum named me after her favourite musician, Fela Kuti. He spoke a lot about the political injustices and he did it with a lot of sass and satire, which made him a household name."

"I heard how Nigeria is nuff strict when it comes to religion." Exclaimed Warren.

"Yeah they do take spirituality seriously over there. All on the buses and billboard posters, they've got phrases like 'Jesus is Lord' and 'God is good'. They are constant reminders of God's presence which – "

Fela was cut off because a black car, with a license plate that said P1MP, had just pulled out from a side road and swerved recklessly in front of them. The driver of the other car was honking and shouting something, Warren shouted something back as if the driver would hear it. They came to the traffic lights and pulled up side by side with the car. The driver was a young black man. He had a female in the passenger seat and a kid in the back, strapped into a baby chair. The woman, who was giving them dirty looks, said something to the driver and they both started laughing. Warren opened his window and started cussing her. All of a sudden the driver got out and started to approach the car.

Sapphire didn't waste any time, the traffic lights were still red but she sped off across the intersection. She looked in her rear view mirror to make sure he wasn't coming after them; there was no sign of him.

"You should have just left it Warren, it wasn't worth it." She sounded heated.

"Nah, but he was acting like we should be afraid of him or something."

Warren returned. "I don't give a damn about who he thinks he is, he can't just cut in front of us like that."

"Being abusive towards him isn't going to solve anything." Sapphire replied sounding more calm.

"Sometimes people need to be confronted." Interjected Fela. "We can't have these guys getting away with whatever they want. If you don't stand up to them they'll walk all over you."

"Sometimes I wanna knock man out. I can't take people swearing after me not showing any respect. It's like when your humble people try to take you for a doormat." Warren still sounded vex.

"Confrontation without humility only leads to violence." said Sapphire.

"So what are you suggesting Sapphire, that I turn the other cheek? You can't do that all the time people won't respect you."

"I understand, what you two are saying," said Sapphire. "Humble people are sometimes perceived to be weak, their kindness may be mistaken for weakness. But what we've got to see is that, it takes strength to hold back and not strike out when we're under attack. Many find it hard to see the wisdom in this, the wise person, on the other hand, knows that fists and guns can't fight the devil. The wise know that the battle goes beyond the physical, it is spiritual battle that needs to be fought with the weapons of God."

"What are these weapons?" asked Fela.

"Faith and prayer." She replied in a matter-of-fact manner. "The Bible say's that vengeance is the Lord's and whether we like it or not that's how He designed it to be. Only He is equipped to fight the devil and deliver us from our enemies."

"You're right though," Replied Fela, as if he had just had a eureka experience. "'Coz Israel didn't have to fight the Egyptians for their liberation, God did it for them. He did it to show us that He has the ability to fight for us and He will when we cry out to Him."

"I pray God can show me how to reach that level of humility," rejoined Warren, sounding doubtful. "Cause I really can't see me being able to do it."

The church was densely packed out with people from all different nationalities. The place resounded with the lively conversation of the people seated around their tables which were laid out in a restaurant formation. The building was adorned with beautiful decorations. Ribbons hung from the ceilings and the tabletops were overlaid with fresh cloths and flowers. Byron, one of the ushers allocated Fela, Sapphire and Warren to their table. Fela walked up to the stage to place his gifts; he had some old clothes in a black bag, as well as his old calculator. He saw a lot of P.C's and computer equipment had been donated, as well as note pads, books, microwaves and all other kinds of electrical equipment and appliances. Sapphire brought her keyboard to donate as well as some clothes, Warren followed behind her bringing some of his old garments as well an old tape player.

Not all the gifts that were donated were second hand. Many people, out of the goodness of their heart, had gone out and bought brand new stuff to donate. *So this must be what Decent meant*, Fela thought to himself, *this must have been what he meant, when he spoke of ujima and co-operative economics. People sharing with one another.*

He looked around to see if he could find his mother anywhere. Fela was shocked to see her sitting by the pots waiting to serve the hungry congregation. She had spent the last few days, cooking and preparing the food that was to be served, he was concerned that she was going to burn herself out.

"Mum, when are you going to rest," said Fela, expressing his concern.

"You've been up late these last few days, slaving over pots and pans when are you going to stop."

"My son, it is better to serve than to be served." She smiled, humoured by the way he was fussing over her. " It is the duty of the King or Queen to serve the people and it is an honour because it makes us more Christ like. Christ himself was the greatest King of all, yet he made himself, but a servant amongst us and he commanded his apostles to do the same." He wanted to dispute what she had said, but he couldn't find any way to refute it.

"Well mum after you've done all of this, I want to see you having a long rest. No more running around."

"I will son," she replied laughing. "I promise you that I'll put my feet up and make you do all the work around the house." They both laughed.

The Pastor had started speaking, so Fela took leave of his mum and went back to his table to be seated.

"...If we want to build as a community it is expedient that we all band together and make a serious effort to change things. A few weeks ago my wife said some encouraging words to me, she said 'Build your hopes on him who can do what to us is impossible'. These words really touched me, because looking around at the state of society, one can sometimes think that there is no hope for the future. It may seem like to make things change for the better will be impossible, but my wife's words showed me otherwise. I believe that many of you in the crowd and others out there, feel that it is impossible for us to make a difference. But today I'm here to tell you, in the words of my wife, that you can

'Build your hopes on God who can do what may seem impossible'.

There were numerous shouts of "Amen", from the crowd, as well as clapping and general shouts of agreement.

"The fact that so many of you are here," Continued the Pastor. "Shows that there are many people out there who do care about our neighbours, even the ones that don't live in the same country as us. I tell you folks, now is the time for action, 'the harvest is plenty but the workers are few'. We need people to be active, even if all you do is find a young person in jail, who you write to, once a month. That is start, or you could go and visit the single mother with three kids, who lives down stairs from you, once a fortnight. These things are all a step in the right direction, they bring us a step closer to achieving a unified, peaceful, godly society. So come along to our meetings, be part of our think tank, we need your support, experience and ideas. But what we need most of all, is your willing hearts." The Pastor ended his speech by telling people where they could get information about various projects and initiatives, then he blessed the food and it was time to eat.

The food on offer comprised of dishes that came from all over the world. Fela sampled many of them, some of which had names he couldn't even pronounce.

Back at his table he enjoyed light conversation with Sapphire, Warren and Alex, a drummer in the church's band. While he was eating an usher came over to alert him to the fact that his performance would be after the dinner.

Just as he was finishing his food, the Pastor called for everyone's attention.

"I would like you all to welcome to the stage a very special friend of mine."

Fela felt a nervous shiver down his spine; he knew it was his time. "He's a poet and he is going to grace us with one of his poems today. I would like to introduce to you, Fela Moore."

At the sound of clapping Fela got up and walked across the auditorium to the stage. He felt more unnerved than ever, the crowd before him was much larger than any crowd he had performed in front of before.

"What's up everyone?" He said shyly.

"Heaven!" Shouted someone in the crowd in reply to his greeting. Laughter bubbled around the room, which helped to ease the tension Fela was feeling in his body. He felt awkward, having so many eyes boring him at once made him feel uncomfortable, like a man lying on a bed of nails.

"This poem I'm going to perform is called…'a New day'." He didn't know what else to say so he launched straight into the poem. It was about the fact that it was time for a new beginning, he had wrote it around the time when he first came out of jail. A new day was a metaphor for a new beginning. He forgot the words half way through, so he restarted. He felt so embarrassed but the crowd didn't seem to mind they just laughed it off. This made him feel more comfortable and he was able to remember the lines he had forgotten. When he had finished the crowd gave him a tremendous round of applause that almost knocked him off his feet. His mother came over and made him feel more uneasy by giving him a big hug and a kiss.

"That was awesome!" Remarked Alex, the drummer, when Fela returned to the table. Sapphire and Warren agreed.

"Was that a new lyric blood?" Asked Warren.

"No, I wrote that when I first got out of jail." He said sipping on some orange juice, (He still hadn't written anything new since his cousin's death, he didn't know why, it just wasn't coming).

"Did I look nervous up there?" He asked them.

"I couldn't tell from here," replied Alex "but you definitely didn't sound nervous." Fela told them that his legs had felt like jelly.

"Why?" enquired Sapphire. "You were ok the other day at the Spice bar."

"Yeah I know, but it was dark in there, I couldn't see all the peoples eyes staring at me, and plus, it was a smaller crowd."

Calvin sat in the back of Shine's ride. Shine, Roach and himself were on their way back to Shine's to weigh some drugs they had just purchased. Ever since finding out about Paul, Calvin was feeling more and more uncomfortable with the life he was living. When he asked Shine if he had heard about Paul, Shine just laughed and said Paul deserved what he got. Since then he was convinced that Shine had something to do with Paul's death and this made him feel very circumspect around him. The dodgy phone conversation he heard him having the other day also served to make him even more wary. Who was Shine speaking to? Did he set Rico up? It was common knowledge that Rico was arrested that same day. Calvin was confused, he couldn't believe, that Shine could be a paid informer, but that's how it looked. It was a mix of intrigue and fear that kept him still working for Shine, he dreaded to think about where it would all end up.

As they were driving Roach spotted a parked car which had P1MP on it's number plate. He made some joke about it, pointing it out to Shine and Calvin who both turned to look at it simultaneously.

"I swear that was Big Mike's baby mother in that car!" Shine exclaimed, not really to anyone in particular. Calvin had heard of Big Mike before but he didn't know how he looked, he had just heard about the beef between him and Shine. The story on the street was that, they used to be partners in crime but somehow jealousy came between them and they became enemies. There were conflicting stories about how the jealousy came about; some say 'it was over gal' others say 'it was over money', the truth is no one really knew how it started but there was definitely a beef between them. They had a big shoot out on Southbury Road once, it was the talk of the town and that was when Calvin first heard about Shine. His school was on fire with rumours about him. People were talking about him like he was a super hero, even though, most of them never even knew him. Calvin, who was just a kid, known for being good at football, saw the respect Shine had and longed for the same. He had never known his father and he had no real solid male role model to look up to. Being pushed around at school was a regular thing for him. He had wished then, that Shine or someone like him was a relation of his, that way, no one would be able to touch him.

"Are you sure that was her?" asked Roach, shocked that Shine was reversing the car. He was Shine's cousin and the only person he moved around with, because to Shine, everyone else was just an associate and not to be trusted.

"There's only one way to find out." replied Shine as he parked up. He got out and walked off into the night towards the vehicle, which was a few yards away. Calvin's heart started racing, he was scared that something was going to happen. He knew Shine always carried his gun and he knew he wasn't afraid to use it. If that was Big Mike's ride then something was going to happen. Roach didn't say anything, he just watched, from where they were they could see everything.

As Shine got closer to the car a man walked out of a nearby off licence carrying a plastic bag. He looked around average height and he had a slim build. *That can't be him*, Calvin thought, *he's not big*. He started to relax but then all of a sudden, Shine who had been hiding by a car, popped up brandishing a hand gun.

He shouted out a curse word which made the man turn his head, just as he was about to enter his car. When the man saw Shine, he dropped everything he was holding and started to run. Shine pursued his prey, firing successive rounds after him. Calvin almost jumped out of his seat. Everything around him became a flurry of confusion. Baby mother getting out of car! Shots being fired! Glass smashing! People shouting! Someone screaming! Roach stayed quiet as he sat watching the whole spectacle in the rear view mirror.

Within no time at all Shine returned to the car, jumped in and before Calvin could catch his breath, they were speeding off down the road. Everything happened so fast, it all seemed like a dream to Calvin, a really bad dream.

"I popped him, I popped him." Shine shouted triumphantly, he was laughing. "I hope he's dead."

"Shine what have you done?" Roach's high pitch voice sounded distressed. "How can you just do that blood? Shine your sick, Shine your—"

"Shut up man!" snapped Shine. "I told you. When I see that guy, I don't care where it is, I'm taking him out. He tried to kill me so I had to get him. It's kill or be killed."

"But Shine there were bare witnesses, do you wanna get us all arrested?" Shine ignored him and turned to Calvin.

"What's wrong Calvin?" He said, looking at him in his rear view mirror, with an evil grin on his face. "You look like you've just seen a murder." He laughed to himself and Calvin saw that demonic look in his eyes again. "Don't worry Calvin, as long as you keep your mouth shut you ain't got nothing to worry about..." Shine's words tormented Calvin as they drove home in silence.

13

The week came when Fela was to start work at the youth club. It had taken a month for his Police check to come through, but finally Brenda received it and gave him the all clear. On his first day he was given the task of supervising some young people who were doing a play on gun crime and how it affects the community. That was a bit of a challenge because Fela had never really been any good at drama but he got through it alright. The young people were mostly polite and helpful although he did get some bad attitude from one young madam. It reminded him of the way he used to treat the teachers when he was at school. It made him see how hard it must have been for some of the teachers, who were trying to teach classes full of difficult kids on their own.

"So how did you find your first day." asked Brenda when they were clearing up at the end.

"It was ok I guess, most of the youth were cool. But there was this one girl called Sasha she was quite challenging."

"Yeah," replied Brenda. "Sasha's got issues, she lives in a care home. She's alright once you get to know her, but you've got to be patient with her. I'll have a talk with her when I see her tomorrow. But apart from that was everything ok?"

"Yeah, more or less." Fela stopped to wave to some of the other workers who were leaving. "The play's coming along nicely, they've really put some good scenes together. I felt useless being there because I can't act and if anything, they were teaching me."

"That's the whole point," Brenda laughed. "It's a learning experience. You can't expect to know it all straight away. You'll develop the necessary skills as you go along. Anyway you seemed to be doing fine to me. I heard you leading them in the discussion on gun crime."

"I didn't start it they did," Fela said, smiling and brandishing his pearly white teeth. "I was just facilitating the discussion. One of them started talking about the shooting two months ago, of that man, Big Mike. I was telling them how gun crime was on the increase and how it is having a negative effect on the wider community. We talked about what factors may have caused an increase in gun crime and how we might be able to curb it. They had a lot to say and we filmed some of it with the camcorder."

She commended him for his work, telling him that it's not often the young people would be up for a discussion like that.

"A lot of young people," she commented. "Don't have an outlet to express their ideas and opinions. So when it comes down to getting their points across in a public setting, they find it hard to open up."

"I know, that's why I was thinking of starting an arts academy," Fela explained. "We could train them to express their many frustrations and aspirations through the arts that they enjoy."

"That's a really good idea," said Brenda. 'The only problem is how would we fund it?"

"We can apply to the government." Fela replied, as they were moving a table. "I have a proposal already written up. My cousin gave it to me before he died and I've made some tiny adjustments to it, so now all we have to do is send it off.

"We've tried that before when we wanted to get some studio equipment but they turned us down." said Brenda.

"We can try again there's no harm in that is there?" Fela asked.

"No I guess not," said Brenda, looking thoughtful. "I tell you what, bring the proposal in as soon as possible."

On his way home Fela was in high spirits, he was excited about the project and he couldn't stop thinking about it. He decided to stop by Ramona's to tell her about it, he wanted her involved in the project, teaching dance.

"How are you Sis?" said Fela, hugging Ramona as he walked through the door.

"Not too good actually," she replied, looking slightly troubled. "Calvin just left and he's acting really weird, he seems shifty. I know Calvin, when he's acting like that it's because there's something wrong and he's trying to hide it from me. I'm really scared for him Fela. When I hear about these shootings my heart starts beating fast and I'm saying 'please don't let it be him, God please don't let it be him'." Fela was quiet. He didn't know how to advice her. Then he remembered a principle, Ade had taught him. It was called 'Question and you will see'. He had said it was the key to understanding a person's dilemma and helping them get through it.

"It sounds like you're doing a lot of worrying, why?"

"I worry," she started, sounding defensive. "Because I'm scared that something's going to happen to my brother."

"But will worrying save your brother?"

"No not necessarily, but by me showing concern it may make him reconsider his actions."

"Would you agree with me if I said showing concern doesn't mean you have to always be worrying about him?"

"Yeah I guess so because showing concern is showing that you care but worrying is stressing yourself out when that person's not even there to witness it."

"Exactly!" exclaimed Fela. "There is a thin line between concern and worry; and it's called sanity. When we cross over from concern to worry we make ourselves sick because we're not meant to worry. We have a God, who is Almighty, if you need anything done just ask it of Him. He may not come when you want Him to but He's always on time. We just need to trust Him. You trying to save Calvin on your own is too big a burden for you to bear. That's why I say let me help, I can speak to him for you."

Ramona agreed to let Fela have a go at trying to speak to Calvin, she figured she had nothing to lose. To make her feel better Fela told her about his plan to start an academy and how he wanted her involved.

"Are you sure that the government are going to fund it though?" she asked, sounding apprehensive. "What if they turn around and say no?"

"There you go worrying again." Fela laughed. "I believe that they will fund it but if they don't, I trust God to provide another way. I truly do believe every problem has a solution."

14

The following day Fela decided to take a trip down to the Express yourself forum and he invited Sapphire along with him. They were always debating issues connected to love and relationships. The forum was addressing this topic, that particular evening and Fela thought Sapphire might be interested in attending.

They arrived late and the debate had already started. The room was filled with approximately thirty people seated in a circle. All heads turned briefly when they entered. Fela was surprised to see so many young people in attendance. At the last session there were only a handful but this time the place was packed out with them. Some of their faces, he recognised from the youth club, he nodded to them as well as Scott. Fela noticed Brenda wasn't with him.

"I would feel awkward asking my man to come to the clinic with me," said a young lady. "it would be like me saying 'I don't trust you'." She was looking into a camera that Fela hadn't even noticed.

"But if he hasn't got nothing to hide, he should

have no problem going with you." Came a voice from across the room. It was accompanied by a brief round of applause.

"If your partner is willing to get checked out with you," said Scott, who was facilitating, "it shows that you can be both open and honest with one another which will help build up trust between you." There were murmurs of agreement amongst the crowd.

"Recently," he continued. "A survey was published which stated that in the last nine years there has been a 57% increase in the contraction of STD's. Can anyone think of any explanation as to why this has occurred?"

"I think it's because people aren't educated enough about how lethal these diseases are." said a brother sitting next to Fela. "Everyone's thinking about the pleasure and not the pain that will come after, it's that laugh now cry later philosophy."

"I think that the media has a lot to do with this increase as well." Said another young lady. "Casual sex is promoted more in our teenage magazines, daytime T.V. and pop songs." Fela raised his hand to speak and Scott prompted him to speak with a nod.

"Without meaning to be controversial," Said Fela, feeling a little nervous, "I want to throw something in the mix here. The problem seems to be promiscuity and not the lack of sex education. In schools young people are educated about the dangers of unprotected sex but because they don't know how to control their desires, they end up committing that irresponsible act. Let's face it young people are too immature to think rationally about "safe sex", most of them just want a quick fix and that's it. Plus these contraceptives don't always work, abstinence is the —"

"Yeah that sounds nice in theory," interjected Scott. "But in the real world, abstinence, isn't practical. We live in a hedonist world and many people see casual sex as a sport, something like bungee jumping, it's dangerous but fun at the same time. What we need to do is protect ourselves from the hazards—"

"But couldn't we say that—" Fela tried to speak, but Sapphire cut him off."

"Yeah but for some," She started. "Speeding down the high road at 100 miles per hour in a 30 mile per hour zone, is their idea of having fun, but most sensible people know how fatally dangerous it really is. It's so dangerous that it's banned yet large numbers of people die from it every year. Where as bungee jumping can only kill the individual, causal sex, like reckless driving can seal the fate of many, all from one senseless act."

"If everyone follows the Highway Code," She continued. "There will be a lot less accidents, if followed, it's a system that will work. Marriage is the same and as the effects of sexual diseases and the break down of the family unit continues to destroy our nation, I pray many people will wisen up and enter into a monogamous relationship. They say 'if it ain't broke don't fix it', there is nothing wrong with the marriage system." There were a few laboured claps from the audience but the general response was one of indifference.

"You speak as if everyone can deal with being in

118

a monogamous relationship." Came a challenge from the boy sitting next to Fela. Fela attempted to answer him but Sapphire cut him off again.

"We can, we won't die if we abstain from having sex. If you need it so bad you can always go out and get married." There were a couple murmurs of approval amongst the congregation.

The facilitator then asked the group why people found it hard to stay in monogamous relations and if there was any such thing as finding your 'soul mate'? The debate was filled with mixed responses but through it all Fela kept quiet. He didn't like the way Sapphire had kept cutting him off and he was going to let her know about it. After the session Scott approached Fela and Sapphire, he was dressed modestly in khakis a white T-shirt with a picture Che Guavera on it.

"Thanks for coming down Fela." He said, sticking his fist out for Fela to touch. Fela, misinterpreting his gesture, stuck his hand out for Scott to shake. After a fair bit of confusion they ended up just shaking hands, and Fela introduced Scott to Sapphire.

"Yeah I really appreciated your input tonight," Scott continued. "You two made some very interesting points. I was wondering if you would like to come down and do a talk on gun culture, Brenda was telling me that you are knowledgeable in that area. I reckon the young people would enjoy it and they would really be able to benefit from your insight."

"Yeah," Replied Fela. "I would definitely be interested in doing that, just give me a buzz and we can arrange something." Fela thought Scott was a cool guy, he didn't like the way he cut him off when he was speaking but he was going to let that slide because he knew that was what facilitators do. Sapphire, on the other hand, was not going to get off so easily. He felt she had disrespected him when she cut him off twice when he was trying to speak and that wasn't the first time. She had a habit of doing it and Fela felt insulted whenever she did.

"That was a really good session don't you think?" Asked Sapphire as they drove home that night. Fela just grunted a response. "It would be really nice to run a session there, wouldn't it?"

"Yeah then you could do all the talking, seeing as that's what you specialise in." He replied, sounding sarcastic. Sapphire was taken aback by his satirical comment.

"What are you talking about?" She asked.

"Well maybe if you stopped cutting me off when I'm speaking you would know ." Fela paused, then continued. "I don't like the way you kept talking over me in there. Every time I tried to make a point, you butted in with one of yours. You were acting like I couldn't speak for myself. Not all of us went to private school like you, so forgive me if I take longer to articulate my sentences." There was an awkward silence before Sapphire finally spoke.

"I'm sorry if I offended you," She started, sounding upset. "I was only trying to back you up." At that moment Fela felt his indignation begin to wane like a fire slowly dying out, but he remained quiet.

"I know I can get carried away at times," she

continued, her brown eyes confirmed that her modesty was bona fide. "But that's just a character flaw of mine, and we all have those."

"I guess so." Fela agreed, releasing his tension with a sigh. "I'm what some may call 'dyslexic' and I find it hard to express myself at times, so it gets frustrating when I'm trying to speak and people cut me off." Sapphire apologised, saying she understood where he was coming from. She admitted that she disliked it when people, in her class at university, would cut her off before she finished debating a point. She could definitely relate to what he was saying.

After it had been established that there were no hard feelings, Fela decided to take his leave of Sapphire. They had been parked outside his house talking for a while and they had been having an intimate conversation. Fela felt they had both been real with each other and he was sure that from what he saw that Sapphire was a genuine woman, the type that he could marry. As he walked into his house he decided that next time he saw her, he would ask her to be his lady.

It was the weekend and Fela was on his way to meet Brenda at the youth club. He was rolling up there with Warren, he was going to introduce him to Brenda as the man he wanted to teach sound engineering at the academy. He had submitted his proposal a few months before and he was confident the government would give him the funds he needed. He was also planning to bring in Ramona when everything was set up. She was definitely going to be the dance teacher; he'd confirmed that with Brenda already.

Things were finally looking up for Fela. He was getting his goals achieved and his career seemed like it was coming together. He felt the only thing left for him to do was to get his soul mate. Sapphire was still his number one candidate; in fact she was his only candidate but he hadn't had a chance to ask her yet. She was in the middle of exams and he wanted to give her the space she needed. He could always wait until after she had finished her exams to tell her how he felt.

As Fela was walking to the BIG Thinking project with Warren, he spotted Calvin on the corner with his boy Tiny. Fela had recently phoned him and tried to speak to him like he promised Ramona he would, but Calvin didn't give him the time of day. He simply stated 'I don't wanna hear it'. Fela didn't want to get into an argument with him so he left him, but he still wanted to reach Calvin, he really believed there was a way.

Fela and Warren stood listening to Tiny emceeing some lyrics to Calvin, and a couple of other young people who were standing around spectating. He was talking some positive stuff; the verse was about how guns were tearing their communities apart. Fela was impressed.

"That was tight bruv!" Fela said, touching Tiny's fist with his own. Everyone else present also showed Tiny some kind of appreciation for what he did. Tiny explained to them that he would be performing the same lyric at the Drayton park festival which was only a couple of weeks away.

"Are you still rhyming, Fela" Asked Tiny.

"Of course!" Affirmed Fela. "I'll even rhyme for you now." Fela then proceeded to teach them some street knowledge. He figured that the best way to reach the youth was through the music. Decent had once told him:

"You have to give the youth what they need to hear dressed up how they want to hear it." He had to communicate with them in their terms, in their language otherwise they wouldn't be able to digest what he was saying.

Fela rhymed them his "A new day" poem and they were all amazed. Some were amazed because they had never heard a rap without any profanity. Others who had the capacity to go deep, were shocked by how deep Fela actually took it. Even Calvin had to clap when Fela finished, he knew he was touched.

"Were you lot feeling that?" Fela asked trying to sound modest.

"Yes!" Exclaimed Tiny sounding ecstatic, he gave Fela a two fists touch.

"That was a big verse, your metaphors were on point and your rhyme schemes were heavy bruv! You need to give me some pointers."

"I can do you one better than that," Fela boasted. "I can get you on this course I'm running. It's going to involve writing music, recording it and performing it. We're looking for rappers, poets, singers and dancers. Who here is interested?"

Tiny and some of the other youth present said they would do it. He took their numbers down, but he was disappointed that Calvin didn't attempt to show any interest.

"Aren't you up for it Calvin?" Fela asked looking into Calvin's troubled eyes. "I remember you to have been a heavy wordsmith back in the day."

Calvin grunted something about not having enough time to emcee anymore. "I have to make my money and run tings out here I ain't got time to sit around in youth clubs." He stated.

"Yeah but bro, you know it's not about that, don't you?" Fela replied, sounding let down. "It's too wicked out here for blessed brothers like yourself to be getting caught up in the game."

"The game may be shiesty but I need to make my money out here." Calvin gesticulated with his hands like he had money in them. "Like they say 'get rich or die trying.' And anyway, who's going to try it with me when I'm rolling with Shine and

Roach? The likelihood that I'll be robbed, beaten or worse, on these streets is next to nothing. The man I roll with run da streets and everything in it." Warren, who had been keeping quiet, decided to speak as if it was his appointed time to do so.

"Young blood there are only three places the streets can take you; jail, an early grave or a life of drug addiction. Is that what you want for yourself?"

"I ain't got nothing to lose," said Calvin getting on his moped. "My life's messed up any way."

"Look Calvin, I can't force you to change," said Fela walking up to the moped. "If you want to change, that's got to come from inside of you. Where there is life there is hope. The living God can help you turn your life around, only if you let Him." Calvin grunted a response, said his goodbyes and sped off on his moped.

15

When Fela reached the youth club the workers were tidying up and most of the young people had left. Hussein, a Turkish man that worked there, notified him that Brenda was in her office.

"What's up Brenda?" he said as he knocked on the door, which was slightly ajar.

"Hi Fela," she replied, looking up from her desk and removing her glasses. "I was going to call you actually I've got a letter for you, I think it's about the funding." Fela's heart started beating fast; he was excited, he knew the funds would come through. He had worked on the proposal arduously, drafting and redrafting it, so he was sure it would be accepted.

"I found it." She said coming over and giving him a white envelope. Fela ripped it open and held his breath as he scanned the page. He then cut the tense silence with a sharp kissing of his teeth.

"They rejected the proposal," he said handing the letter to a concerned looking Brenda. "I can't believe they rejected the proposal." He pounded his fist into his palm. He felt like a man who had betted all he had on one horse and lost it all.

"What am I going to do now?" Fela said looking up at the sky.

"Keep on trying," replied Warren. "Just keep on sending them your proposal. That way, they will know you're serious. They'll just give you the funds, to stop you hassling them."

"But that will take too long I need to start this academy now, this community needs it.

"You could do a fundraiser to gain the communities support for what you're doing." The cogwheels in Fela's mind had come to an abrupt halt when he read the letter but now they started to turn again. He thought of how successful the gala at his church had been, he wanted to do something like that. He decided that he would speak to the Pastor about getting the church members to help put some funds towards his project. *After all*, he thought, *Christianity is about charity*.

"Fela I think it's a great idea," said Pastor Blake, the next day at church, after Fela had finished telling him his plan. "What I'm going to do is confer with some of the other local churches to see if we can raise some funds between us to support your cause. Leave me with the proposal so I can show it to them but in the meantime be praying and also think about getting a sponsored walk organised." Fela liked the idea of a sponsored walk and he agreed to try his best to organise one.

It had been two weeks since Fela had spoken with the Pastor about the fundraiser and since then he hadn't had much success. Getting sponsors was proving to be a harder task than he thought it would. Brenda had rounded up some of the youth from the club to get sponsors, but they hadn't been too serious about it. Some of the local churches where involved in the sponsoring, but little money had been raised. Fela was feeling defeated. Not only was his idea for the academy being hindered, but on top of that he found out that Sapphire was going to be travelling to Grenada that week. When he found out her exams had finished he met up with her and was ready to tell all, but she told him her news first. He felt frustrated, now he would have to wait till she returned before he told her anything.

Ramona had been asking him for a while to follow her to see Shaun in jail. He had been turning her down because he just didn't feel ready to re-visit the place yet, but now he felt he was, so when she asked he agreed to go with her.

When he arrived at the jail, Fela was immediately pronged by bad memories. Lonely nights in a cell, fights, screaming, anger and despair haunted his recollections like ghosts. He saw Shaun sitting at the desk waiting for them. He was a hard faced character with a bushy afro and stubble beard. He smiled as they approached him displaying his missing front tooth.

"Mr Moore," he pressed his fist against the glass in front of him. "It's good to see you." His voice sounded rough and weary through the jail house phone. They talked for a few minutes just about how the jail was reminiscing on the old times. Fela could feel that things weren't the same, he was changing and apart from old memories they didn't really have anything to talk about. Shaun was still on a quest for street fame and riches; he hadn't learnt his lesson, instead he had become more hard headed.

Ramona and Kenya were with Fela and they both had their turn to speak to him as well. Calvin wasn't with them because he hated Shaun. Once when Calvin was eleven he got into a fight with Shaun who was beating up Ramona. Shaun would have scattered him if the police had got to the house any later. Ramona refused to press charges and accepted Shaun back after that, this caused a rift between her and the rest of her family. Shaun never repeated his act of violence again but he replaced beating with cheating and Ramona still kept him. Even Fela, who had known him since they were kids, had to cut him off for a while because Shaun ended up in bed with one of his girlfriends.

After Ramona and Kenya had their turn to speak, they were ready to leave. The prison guard took Shaun back to his cage and the trio headed back home.

"I guess being in there must have brought back some painful memories?" Ramona asked as they rode the train home.

"Yeah it brought back some but nothing more painful than seeing your boy locked up, especially when it looks like he don't want to change." Fela didn't want to bad mouth Shaun to his baby's mother but he felt exasperated and he needed to let it out.

"I know what you mean," replied Ramona, to Fela's surprise, she was normally so defensive of her man. "I wish he could be more like you, I'm not saying you're prefect but at least you made a decision to do the right thing."

"I'm trying," said Fela, modestly. "It is a process and I have faith that Shaun will change but until then we just have to lead by example and wait for our loved ones to follow suit."

16

Calvin stood blazing in the flats on Drayton Park Estate, he was waiting for Shine to come and deliver him a package. As he was waiting he saw a black tinted jeep pulling up on the ground below him. The door opened and a cloud of smoke was released from the car followed by none other than Shine! Shine stood by the door of the vehicle talking to someone inside. It was late at night so Calvin couldn't really see properly, but he did glimpse the hand of a Caucasian man passing Shine something. Shine took whatever it was and put it in his jacket pocket and the jeep reversed back out of the estate beeping in the process. Calvin watched Shine whip out his phone and dial then he suddenly felt his phone vibrating, it was Shine.

"Where are you?" Shine sounded irritated.

"I'm in the flats, I'm coming now." Calvin said nervously. Shine swore and put the phone down. Calvin rushed down the stairs because the lift was taking long. He didn't want to keep Shine waiting, the last time he did he got a black eye for it. Since the murder incident Shine had been extremely touchy, he was always on edge and any little irritation was likely to trigger his anger. Deep inside Calvin was scared. No one had called his name in relation to the murder but it was only a matter of time he suspected.

By the time Calvin reached him, Shine had already climbed into his car. Calvin opened the door and got in, and as he did so Shine punched him in the face and grabbed him by the throat.

"What are you trying to take me for?" Shine was shouting and spitting as he spoke. He spluttered out sordid verbal abuse in-between claims that Calvin was trying to take him for a fool. He accused Calvin of coming up short with his money and he made all kinds of wicked threats. Calvin was afraid, his heart was beating fast and tears started to stain his cheeks.

"Stop being a muppet," snapped Shine. "dry your eyes before I give you something to really cry about." He let go of Calvin's neck and allowed him to dry his eyes. Shine reached in his pocket and Calvin's eyes screamed, he thought he was going to be shot.

"What are you getting scared for?" laughed Shine, handing him an ounce of weed. "If I was going to do you some harm I would have done it long-time. If you don't want trouble just make sure when I ask you for my money you have all of it for me."

"Yes Shine," replied Calvin. "I'll have your money for you ASAP." The truth was that Calvin had always given Shine all his money so he didn't understand what Shine was on about.

"Make sure you have my papers when I phone you."

Shine uttered one last warning as Calvin climbed out of his car and got onto his moped. Calvin was about to reply when he heard, what sounded like fireworks going off.

POW! POW! POW!

When he heard the sound again a nearby car window smashed and Calvin knew that it was not fireworks but gun shots that were being let off. Without warning Shine reversed and sped off, a shot was let off again. Calvin turned the key on his moped. *Nothing !* His heart was beating fast. Another shot rang out and rebounded off a wall next to Calvin. With shaky hands Calvin tried the key again; the engine hummed. Calvin revved the bike and jetted off.

Ramona sat watching T.V. in her living room. She was watching a romantic comedy but it was reminding her of how lonely she was so she changed the channel. She flicked through a couple of her favourite networks but there was nothing on that interested her. She looked at the clock; *half-past midnight.* It was time for her to go to bed but as she got up the doorbell rang.

"Who is it?" she called aggressively.

"It's me Calvin." Came the sorry reply.

"Calvin?" she said opening the door. "Do you know what time it is?"

"I needed somewhere to go, I was being chased." He sounded out of breath and his eyes looked terrified.

Ramona felt pity in her heart but she couldn't help being annoyed.

"Who's chasing you? I hope you're not going to bring trouble to my doorstep Calvin? I've got a baby in here remember."

"No one followed me." Calvin sounded irritated. "I don't even know whether they were shooting at me or Shhh — my friend." Calvin was about to say Shine's name then he remembered that Ramona didn't know he was rolling with Shine. He hadn't told her in case Ramona tried to do the big sister thing and approach Shine.

"I told you not to get yourself involved with thugs but you never listened."

Ramona was sitting down and Calvin was standing yet he still felt like she was talking down to him. There was a silence and they both heard the sound of police sirens in the distance.

"Calvin can't you see that this life isn't worth it?" Ramona's eyes looked like they were pleading. "Can't you see that you're putting yourself and your family in serious danger here? I wanna help you but if you're not ready to help yourself then what can I really do for you? Why don't you just give it all up?"

"I can't," said Calvin turning his head to avoid her gaze. "I feel like I'm at the point of no return." Ramona got up, walked over to him and held his hands in hers.

"Its never too late Calvin." He looked up to meet her hope filled eyes, they looked watery.

"But you don't understand how deep I am in this."

"How can I understand if you don't tell me what's going on?"

"I can't." Calvin looked away.

"Why?"

"Because I need to deal with this on my own. It's a man's world and I need to learn to fend it for myself."

17

The day of Drayton Park festival arrived. The park was buzzing and alive with the sound of music and celebration. Locals and aliens alike were gathered to take part in the day's festivities. Fela walked through the crowd carrying Kenya, closely followed by Ramona and Warren. Ramona took Kenya to go on some rides so Fela and Warren decided to take a stroll around the park. There were so many activities going on, from face painting to dance competitions. Fela was happy to see there were no problems, so far all was peaceful. The festival had a reputation for being rowdy, so there was always a strong police presence.

The last time Fela attended was just before he went to jail and it was an unforgettable experience for him. Shaun, himself and some of the local boys he used to move around with got into a skirmish with some "out-of-towners". When the police came running over everyone split. As they were running Fela noticed a pain in his leg. When he looked down he saw his trouser leg covered in blood; he had been stabbed.

He went to the hospital and had to have his thigh stitched-up. He never saw the boys again but for a long time he wanted revenge. Whilst in jail, when he became a Christian, Ade sent him a tape on forgiveness. Listening to the tape made him see things in a different light, if God could forgive us we had to forgive others. 'Do onto others as you want done unto yourself' Ade had told him, he knew then that he had to forgive.

Now he was at the festival with a different mentality. He had a different perspective from what he had then, a paradigm shift had occurred; the cup was half full not half empty. Even though some bad things had happened to him Fela was determined not to let that stifle his progress. He was talking with Warren about his plan for them to make a music album with his production, when he heard a familiar voice calling him. Fela turned round and saw Tiny standing behind him.

"You know I'm performing in about five minutes," said Tiny, after touching fist with Fela and Warren. " I hope you're coming!?"

"Yeah I'm gonna be there," replied Fela. "Where is it?"

"Come," suggested Tiny. "You might as well follow me cause I'm going there now." When they arrived at the stage there was a large crowd already gathered around that area. On stage some young people were dancing and Fela marvelled at the level of talent that was being display. He felt more determined than ever to do something, so that the talented youth could showcase their talents in a positive way.When the dancing ended, the host called Tiny onto the stage. Tiny appeared looking self-assured, as the crowd welcomed him on. As soon as he started emceeing the crowd went crazy, so the DJ had to rewind the tune. They did this three times, because the people loved it so much.

✦　　✦　　✦

"Ain't that Calvin?" asked Roach, as he and Shine were walking through the crowd in Drayton Park. Shine turned his head in the direction Roach was pointing in.

"Where?" returned Shine.

"Over there," Roach pointed again. "That boy in hooded-top next to the trees."

"The one talking to that tall brother?"

"Yeah, it looks like him." They decided to walk over to see if it was him, from where they were standing they couldn't see the face properly. Shine was vexed. If it was Calvin he was going to hurt him. The customers had been phoning him saying that they couldn't get through to Calvin's line. Shine then tried him but the phone kept on going to voicemail. He thought Calvin had turned his phone off, so he could sneak to the festival.

✦　　✦　　✦

"What's going on Fela?" asked Calvin as the tall young man approached him.

"I'm cool, how about yourself?" replied Fela.

"I'm good, just maintaining."

"Your sister's here with Kenya."

"Yeah I know," replied Calvin, listlessly. "I was with them earlier for a little while."

"I just spoke to her she's over by the rides still," continued Fela, ignoring

Calvin's uninterest. "I'm going to meet her now, you might as well come." Calvin declined Fela's offer saying he had to leave.

"Did you see Tiny's performance?" Fela asked.

"Yeah, that performance was big." Calvin tried to sound lively but Fela could see that he wasn't happy.

"Is everything alright with you Calvin?" inquired Fela. "You seem down."

"Nah, I'm cool." Calvin lied, he couldn't bring himself to tell anyone about the things he had on his mind. He had witnessed a murder, he'd been beaten up by Shine and shot at. He wanted someone to talk to, but he was afraid of what Shine would do if he found out. He remembered the chilling warning Shine had given him, after he murdered Big Mike: 'as long as you keep your mouth shut you ain't got nothing to worry about'. The words still echoed clearly in his mind. He was convinced Shine was the devil in the flesh, and he wasn't prepared to put any level of wickedness past him.

"I hope you thought about what we discussed." Fela said looking serious. Calvin suspected Ramona had told him about how scared he had been the other night. It was typical of her, she told Fela everything.

"Yeah, I thought about it but—"

"Oi Calvin," Fela and Calvin turned both at the same time to come face to face with the menacing countenance of Shine. His dark face had contorted into a picture of unmasked fury, a lot like a gorilla that's about to hurt an unsuspecting jungle explorer who's been messing with it's cubs. "Why is your phone off?" Shine's eyes bore into Calvin like daggers.

"It's not," protested Calvin as he brought out the phone. It was off! "The battery must have died without me –"

POW!

Shine's fist put a full stop to Calvin's sentence but before Shine could swing anymore punches Fela came between them.

"Whoa, whoa allow dat bruv," Fela pleaded. "Whatever the problem is I'm sure that we can sort it out in a much better way than this." A crowd of onlookers gathered round to observe the altercation.

"Come out of my way fool." said Shine with a sneer on his face, he was grabbing Calvin's jumper. "Don't make me hurt you." Roach moved forward and gave Fela a violent shove that knocked him off balance. As Fela fell back he threw his arms up in the air to keep his balance and hit Shine in the mouth accidentally. The tension in the air thickened and time seemed to freeze as Shine paused to touch his lip—it was bleeding!

"I'm sorry 'bout dat bro I never meant to—" Fela didn't get to finish his apology. Shine grabbed Fela, head-butted him and kneed him in his stomach. Fela fell to the ground.

"What, did you think I would let you spark me and get away with it!?" Shine's eyes were ignited with rage. He reached inside his jacket and pulled out—the mouth of murder!

All of a sudden time stood still for Fela. Confronted by the barrel of the gun, he became paralysed with fear. It was as if he was looking into the eyes of a cobra. Terror seized him and his mouth became parched, so that all he could do was plead with his eyes. For a split, second everything around him became obscured, and the barrel of the gun became a tunnel, a passage way to...

"DOOM!" Shouted the gun, as it popped off.

A flock of birds that were perched in a nearby tree scattered into the sky as the sound of the gun blast reverberated. As Fela's body lay crumpled on the ground, Shine and Roach made their getaway amongst the screaming crowd, that was dispersing in every direction. Within no time two police officers were on the scene one of which was a Negro the other was Asian. The Asian police officer radioed for an ambulance whilst the Negro policeman applied pressure to Fela's chest wound.

"Did anybody see what happened here?" asked the Negro police officer.

There was an awkward silence as the remaining few observers started to walk away.

"This is why things like this happen," shouted the Asian officer. "No one wants to say anything, so criminals are allowed to get away scot-free. How are you going to stop these senseless crimes, if no one is brave enough to stand up for what's right?" As he spoke Calvin emerged from behind the bushes where he had been hiding.

"I saw what happened." He walked over to the officers. "I saw everything."

✦ ✦ ✦

Lola Moore's house had become a fortress of prayer. Fela had been in a coma for seven days since he had been shot and all throughout the week Lola's Christian friends would stop by to pray for her son. When Sapphire arrived at the house it was a Saturday night and around a dozen people were there crying out to God on behalf of Fela.

"How is he?" asked Sapphire as she stepped through the door. She had returned from her holiday a week early when she heard the news.

"The doctors are saying he's still not in the clear," replied Lola, with tears in her eyes. "They are still keeping him on life support. We're just trusting in the Lord for a miracle." Fela's mother started to weep as Sapphire consoled her. The phone started to ring and Mrs Moore went to answer it.

When she returned the tears were no longer flowing but her eyes were still watery.

"That was the police," she said to Sapphire. "They say that they've arrested the person who they believe may have shot my son. He is also under arrest on another charge for murder. May God help us". Mrs

Moore started crying again. Sapphire and Ramona both comforted her.

They went into the living room where everyone was praying, there were around 15 people. She told them what the Police had said.

"We must not give up hope," shouted one man, who stood up waving his finger. "The Lord is on our side, justice will prevail." There were shouts of Amen and other agreements. The man then went on to read from James 5:16:

'The effectual fervent prayer of a righteous man availeth much.'

"Brothers and Sisters," he continued. "What we are doing here is not in vain, these are not empty words we speak. The Bible promises our faithful prayer will overcome much strife. We have to believe that this attack of the enemy will not prevail. You have to cry out to God with an expectancy and He will answer you." The man's words seemed to recharge everyone's praying power. The whole room once again resounded with the sound, of people earnestly crying out to God, including Mrs Moore, Sapphire and Ramona.

After the prayer session Mrs Moore had to go to the hospital, so she left Ramona in charge of the house and went with Sapphire to go to see Fela at the hospital. Ramona was staying there with Kenya and Calvin because she feared for her life. She was afraid that Shine would come looking for Calvin at her place.

When everyone had finally left Ramona decided to get some sleep, it had been a long day. She had participated in an all night prayer vigil the night before, so her body was feeling weighed down with sleepiness. Calvin had already crashed out, he had been down at the police station for a couple of hours answering questions. After tucking Kenya in, and tidying up around the house, Ramona was about to lay down to sleep when the phone rang.

"Hello." Said Ramona

"Ramona," said the voice. "This is….Auntie Lola." Ramona's heart started beating fast, and her eyes started to swell with tears. Fela's mother sounded like she was crying and her voice was breaking up.

"What's wrong auntie?" asked Ramona, anxiously. "Is everything alright?"

"My dear….all is well, these tears…. these are tears of joy, F-F-F…Fela has come out of the coma!" Ramona dropped the phone and leapt in the air shouting praises to God. Something took control of her, and before she knew it she had woken up Calvin and Kenya.

"Sorry auntie," She said when she finally picked up the phone again. "I'm just so happy to hear, that God has answered our prayers."

"Don't apologise…. don't…. child, go ahead…. praise God," Came the tearful reply. "It was the praises of the Israelites that brought down the walls of Jericho. Just keep praying in faith because we still haven't finished, he is not totally restored yet." Ramona agreed and they said a prayer of thanksgiving together then they ended the call.

18

Ramona stood next to Warren on the podium, Warren had just finished giving his testimony now it was her turn. Pastor Blake called her to step up to the pulpit. She felt nervous but she managed to stay calm and collected.

"I've come here today, to give my life to the Lord." She said glancing down at the piece of paper in her hand. She had prewritten her testimony so as not to forget all there was to say. She heard her daughter shouting, "mummy, mummy" in the background, it reminded her that there were people supporting her in the crowd.

"Like Warren, I made the decision," she continued. "After I saw the miraculous way God healed Fela." She stopped to wipe a tear from her eye. "Even the doctors said they couldn't explain how he pulled through, he stopped breathing twice. But our God came through and turned our sorrow into joy."

"My mother brought me up in the Christian faith but as a teenager I rebelled for various reasons.

However, no matter how much I tried to run I could never escape my mothers prayer. She was always on her knees for my brother and me and I always marvelled at how strong it made her." She paused to wipe her eyes. "Now she is not here but I still have the legacy she handed down to me and lately I've been following her example and praying and it has been working. I've seen God make changes in my life I never thought possible and after what he did for Fela I felt it only right that I dedicate my life to him. But before I do so I just want to say a short prayer to end my testimony." She read out the prayer from her paper:

> "Oh Lord dear God, I thank you for sending Jesus to die for my sins. I ask Lord that you take my broken heart in your hands and shape it to suit your purpose. Give me the strength to be a better woman and allow me to draw closer to you every day of my life. Teach me how to walk in your ways so I can become a Shining star on this earth. In Jesus' name I've prayed. Amen."

"In a little while I'm going to pray for Ramona and Warren," said Pastor

Blake. "But first, I would like to invite someone to come up and speak. Would Fela Moore please make his way to the stage please." There was a round of applause as Fela made his way up the isle on crutches.

Some of the ushers rushed to help him as he climbed up the steps of the podium. When the clapping had subsided, Pastor Blake asked Fela to share some of his testimony with the congregation.

"I'm so happy to be gathered here with you today." There was a brief round of applause and praises to God. "I'm so pleased to join you in celebration as our brother and sister dedicate their lives to God, on this glorious day." Fela was speaking with a level of eloquence he was not accustomed to. He felt like a preacher on the stage and the more the crowd encouraged him the more his confidence grew.

"As you all know," he continued. "I had a near death experience recently when I was shot in the chest. It was only by the grace of God and because of your diligent prayers that I'm able to stand here in front of you today." There were more shouts of Amen and Hallelujah. "It was my miraculous healing that inspired these two to want to know Christ as their personal Lord and Saviour. This shows that no matter what situation you are in, God can turn it around and use it for his glory. Out of a *test* he'll give you a *test*imony and out of a *mess* he'll give you a *mess*age." He turned to face Ramona and Warren.

"For you two, the road ahead is not going to be easy. Trials and tribulations are going to come your way, but you can do all things through Christ who strengthens you. Also the encouragement you'll get from other church members, will help you get through all kinds of hardships. Are we our brother and sister's keepers? Yes, we all have a duty as members of the

148

community to look out for each other. Our fight against poverty, crime and injustice has just begun. I say our fight because these things have an effect on all of us. We can't keep sweeping these problems under the carpet, that won't make them go away. We need to address these things; each with a commitment and dedication like no-other. We need to make this world a better place for our kids to live in, may none of us deny them that right. United we stand divided we fall, remember that. Thank you." When Fela finished his speech there was an uproarious round of applauds from the crowd. People were shouting, dancing and worshipping as everyone joined in chorus to sing songs of praise to God.

✦　　✦　　✦

Calvin sat on a plane looking out of the misty window. They had just taken off and he looked at the land he was leaving regretfully. He was going to miss his old friends, his sister, his neighbourhood – but he had no other choice. Going to Canada was the only way he could escape Shine. He was sure now that Shine definitely had some dodgy deal with some corrupt police officers, he should have known he wouldn't get convicted. All he could do now was hope and pray that nothing bad would happen to his sister, because of his careless actions.

✦　　✦　　✦

Shine leaned back in his ride counting up some papers. They were all red notes; an unambiguous symbolism of the fact that it was all blood money. He was feeling smug, he knew all the charges were going to be dropped, his connections in law enforcement always took care of him so he never had to worry about jail. As he reached in his pocket to put away the money he had just counted, he didn't see the masked figure behind him brandishing a knife. In fact he never realised there was anyone there, until the knife was buried in his neck. He let out a stifled cry as he turned, clutching his bloody neck. He thought he had come face to face with the grim reaper himself, till the masked figure took off their hood and mask to reveal their true identity.

Donna! Shine could not speak, but his eye's said it all. Paul's baby mother nodded her head as if she read his mind. Her face was bony and pale, with spotty, wrinkled skin stretched across it. She wore a mocking expression. It was payback time.

Shine had burst into her house with some other men and kidnapped Paul. When they found him in the park he had been pumped with an overdose of heroin. The coroners report had showed that there was no way Paul overdosed on his own, "he was helped" they said. Since then Donna had been planning to get Shine, she knew that he was the one responsible for her baby father's death.

"The other day I tried shooting after you but I missed." She sneered. "Today I used a knife to make sure I did the job properly." She raised the blood stained knife, then, for Shine, everything went black.

✦   ✦   ✦

Fela lay awake in his bed. He had being trying to catch an afternoon nap but his mind just refused to shut down. A stream of thoughts and memories kept on flooding his mind so that each new thought made him forget about the previous one. First, at the sound of hearing children playing outside, his mind re-wound back to his childhood days. The programs he used to watch, the games he once enjoyed playing and the friends he had. Thinking about his childhood and coming to the reality of the way things were at that present time made him cringe. Things had changed so much in a way he never dreamed they would as a child. Who would have thought that most of the girls he went to school with would become single-mothers, who would have guessed that most of the boys he grew up with, would be dead or in jail. His situation was no better, he was an ex-convict, that's not what he wanted to be when he was a child. He wanted to be a doctor, a lawyer or an astronaut (he could never make up his mind which) but somewhere along the road his dreams died. All was not lost though and he knew it; he still had his testimony. God had answered the prayers of his family and friends by preserving his life. This made him feel special, like he was living proof that Jehovah was God. His was faith was more than a religion, it was a personal relationship that was

151

based on experience. He remembered explaining it to Decent when he came to visit him whilst he was still in hospital:

"You know," he started. "Christianity is so much more than a religion to me."

"How?" asked Decent with a smile, happy to see his young friend had not lost his enthusiasm for a good argument.

"Well," started Fela meditatively. "I can honestly say, not only do I believe in God but I know Him. My faith in God is not based on religious teachings. I have had a personal encounter with God as I've experienced His touch in different areas of my life. You can't see the wind but you know it's there because you see how leaves are blown by it. In the same way, although I can't see God, I know He is there because I've experienced him moving over my life as He works on the inside, making me a new person by changing my heart and the way I think."

"This near death experience taught me the value of life and has made me feel like I'm still alive for a reason or I would not have survived. I feel like God brought me through this to open my eyes to the fact that I'm still alive for a reason because I have a mission on this earth. Not only that, but the Bible is a book of Prophecy, and we see the prophecies are coming to pass. Even deeper still, the in-depth understanding of God's character is unmatched by all the other faiths showing these people had a real relationship with God. What's more the Bible promises us all that we can have the same relationship, we just have to test the evidence." Fela paused to gather his thoughts. "There is always gonna be room for doubt and contradicting arguments that seem to make sense, but that room for doubt is what we are meant to fill with faith…"

"Fela!" Fela's thoughts, were disrupted by his mother's knock at the door. "Is it okay for me to come in?"

"Yeah!"

When his mother entered, she had an awkward smile on her face.

"There's… err … there's … someone here to see you." As the words left her mouth, she stepped out of the way, and from behind the door appeared non other than…

19

"Dad?!" The word was not meant to have left Fela's mouth, it was a private thought.

"Hello Fela." his Dad said, after a short awkward silence. His Father's voice sounded familiar to Fela, but it was too long ago for him to distinguish whether his father's accent had become heavier or not. Although he had lost most of the hair on his head and he had obviously seen younger days, he looked more or less the same as he did in the photo Fela used to have of him. Fela did not resemble his father at all. His father was short, he was tall; his father was chubby, he was skinny; his father was light, he was dark. The only thing they had in common was their surname.

Ola Moore stood for a moment and looked at his son. His eyes looked sad but he had an expression of determination imprinted on his face.

"Well, I'll leave you two to talk." said Lola, breaking the silence, then she left the room, closed the door and…silence.

Fela sat up in his bed, trying to control his resentment.

"Why did you come here?" he said turning his face, in anger.

"I...I...I was... I just wanted to see you...and how you were keeping." His father edged forward.

"Why, you never cared before?" Fela fired at him with his words and his eyes.

"Look," his father let out a sad sigh. "I can't make up for the past, and that's not what this visit is about. I know I've failed you... and it's because of my failure, that I've come to ask for your forgiveness. Even if you won't forgive me, I still want to apologise—"

"Apologise? What is apologising gonna do? You should have been there. It's too late for sorry excuses now..."

Fela began to weep. Tears of anger issued from one eye, tears of grief from the other. His tears so overwhelmed him that he did not see his fathers tears as he came closer to him.

"I'm sorry, I'm so sorry." Said his father solemnly as he knelt by Fela's bed.

Fela did not know why but he raised his arms and put them round his father. Was he trying to strangle him? No, he was hugging him. *No, this can't be right*, he thought, *This was not how I imagined it would be*. He had always imagined that when he met his father again, he would shout at him and that time he would be the one to walk away, out of his life. He was now confused, why was he hugging his father and letting his father hug him. It did not make sense to him, but it felt right.

He had almost died, which made him realise, that life was too short to hold grudges. They are like dark clouds that obscure a sunny sky. As he opened up his arms to his father, he was releasing himself from years of anger and pain.

After a long talk and even longer silences, his father took his leave of him. Fela was left feeling, what would best be described as, liberated.

For many years after his father left, he had carried guilt inside him. Somewhere deep in his heart, he had felt that it was because of him, that his mother and father had separated. In anger, his mother had once lashed out at him, saying that having him was a mistake. Although she never meant it, and later apologised; her words stuck with him. That coupled with the fact that he had been abandoned by his father made him feel unwanted, and in turn a feeling of self-hate began to build up with in him.

Now however, he knew he was not to blame. He had been an innocent child, born into pre-determined circumstances. He felt like a big weight had been lifted from his heart.

"Back then Fela," his father said to him. "Me and your mother...we were both immature and ill prepared for the struggles we were going through. I was insecure...I thought your mother did not respect my presence around the house. I felt robbed of my manhood when I lost my job and...the drink...it became...an escape for me. When I realised what I had become I couldn't bare to be around you or your mother. I could not control myself, and I didn't want to destroy your lives like I was destroying mine."

When Fela later recalled his fathers words, he understood them more than he did at the time of his father's visit. At that time his emotional state would not allow him to. On reflection though, he could see where his old man was coming from. He knew what it was like to be insecure and he was no stranger to the feeling of emasculation; to feel robbed of one's manhood.

He remembered how his father had started to become more and more distant, till he hardly ever saw him. He remembered how he would try to sit on his dad's lap, on the rare occasion when he would be at home, and his dad would send him to his mother. That used to pain him. The man practically neglected him.

He could tell however, that his father was truly sorry for what he had done, by the way he spoke to him. It was more like a friend that had let him down, rather than the big authoritarian figure he had always imagined him to be.

After his father had left him and his mother, (for some woman he met at a bar who subsequently milked him drier than a cow in a famine), he was driven to despair, and he even attempted suicide.

"I was such a failure, I couldn't even get that right." His father said with a remorseful laugh, as he spoke about the suicide attempt. He had taken an overdose of anti-depressants and collapsed in his flat. That same afternoon the Bailiffs, unaware of the circumstances, had come round to collect some furniture. When they arrived they kicked off his door and found him sprawled out on the kitchen floor. They immediately called for an ambulance—they were not going to let him get away that easy.

"After that incident," his father explained. "I had to call my half-brother in Nigeria, to come and bail me out. He is rich, and heads an oil company out there."

"So what happen then?" Fela forced the question out. He had not spoken during his father's discourse, save the occasional prompt. He did not totally understand why his father had told him all he did. Maybe it was guilt or maybe he just wanted Fela's pity. It was not clear. However, Fela listened anyway to see what he could learn about his father's character and whether he was trust worthy. His round face and dark sorrowful eyes made him appear to be innocent enough but Fela had to be sure. Also the shock of just seeing his father after all those years of separation, kept him both speechless and intrigued.

"My brother paid off my debts, booked a flight for me to go to Nigeria and brought me into the company. I've been working there ever since."

There was a question Fela was burning to ask him.

"So, you have any other children?"

"Yeah," his father said breaking eye contact. "I have two girls and I've got another one on the way."

"Oh." Was all Fela could say in reply. He had always wanted other siblings, but not under these circumstances.

To change the subject which was obviously awkward for both of them, his father started to probe him about his life. Fela was not feeling it. He felt tired and his life story was too much to go into, at that moment in time.

"Well I guess we'll catch up some other time." His father held out his hand and Fela embraced it. He sensed that it had been enough for one day and got up ready to leave. Fela got up from his bed and followed his father down the stairs, calling his mother from her room on his way down.

"Thanks again Lola for allowing me to come by." He was walking away and trying to avoid her gaze.

"Thank you for coming by." She smiled pleasantly at him trying to be as friendly as the circumstances permitted.

"Fela, give me a call whenever you feel up to it, yeah."

"Yeah, will do." Replied Fela, in a tone that sounded unsure.

"How did it go?" his mother asked, after she shut the door. He then relayed to her most of what they had talked about, being careful to miss out parts that might have been too painful for her to hear.

"I hope you're not mad at me, for allowing him to turn up unexpectedly like that, I didn't even know he was coming myself. He found out about what had happened to you through one of our relatives and because we've lived in this house ever since…well he knew where to find us I guess."

"No mum, don't worry about it, I'm cool. I learnt a lot from him which made me understand a lot about myself, and why I did certain things. You know, why I was so rebellious, growing up."

"You've come to understanding the underlying issues that were affecting you, uh?" his mother asked knowingly—she then added. "Are you gonna call him?"

"I don't know, most probably, when I've been able to define what he means to me, and what kind of role we can play in each others' lives." He paused and looked at his mother. She smiled as if in anticipation of what he was going to say next. "Mum, I just wanna say I love you, and I appreciate everything you are doing and have done for me."

"Aw, Fela my dear son," she said embracing him. "I love you too and I'm so proud of you."

20

The crowd spilled into the large football arena. As Fela stood on the raised platform, in the middle of the pitch, he couldn't believe what he was seeing. Thousands had turned out, to see the charity football match between, the Drayton Park FC players, far more than he predicted. He had led the march--still on crutches--from Drayton Park to the football stadium, as it was being filmed live for the national news. What he had first anticipated to be a flop was now proving itself to be successful beyond what Fela could have ever imagined.

Jermain Patterson, a young boy from the Big Thinking project, had wanted his uncle, Gavin Patterson, to sponsor him for the sponsored walk. However Gavin being a player for Drayton Park FC wanted to do more, when he heard about what the project was promoting. He was a local lad, who used his talents to keep himself out of trouble and he really liked the idea of teaching young people to do something positive with their gifts. Organising a charity football match, was his way of giving back to the community. All the money made from the tickets was to go to the BIG thinking project. Seeing as their favourite team playing a friendly, gave many the incentive they needed to support the event, many of the local churches took part in the march as well, which was why the numbers were so high.

As Fela prepared to read his poem "Ujima" he took a deep breath. *So this is making it*, he thought to himself. If only Ade could seem him now. The thought vexed him, then he remembered, that in heaven, everyone's life would be viewed so Ade would get to see it on replay. Also not only was his mother and all his friends watching but God was also watching—he had to represent to the fullest.

In front of him, he had the largest audience he had ever performed in front of and he was about to effect all their destinies with his words. He was nervous so he took a deep breath and prayed in his mind for confidence. Then he dedicated the verse to Ade and launched into the performance.

✦   ✦   ✦

When the poem was done the round of applause that he got sounded to him like thunder. Exhilaration ran through his body like an electric shock from lightning bolt.

"Thank you," said Pastor Blake taking the mic from Fela. "This is a man, I have deep respect for, and so would all of you, if you knew what he had been through to get this far." He put his arm around Fela's shoulders while he shared Fela's testimony with the people. The way they cheered for him at the end, made him feel like a hero.

Sapphire was helping the witness team, hand out flyers to the crowd. Fela approached her and called her to the side. He was ready to tell her how he felt. He had prayed about it and he believed it was what he needed to do.

"What's wrong?" Sapphire asked looking a bit anxious.

"I...I...I need to tell you something." Fela felt like he had a bird in his stomach; the wings of love were fluttering inside him.

"What is it?

"Well, what I need to say is...I'm in love with your spirit and I was wondering if we could possibly try to start a relationship." There was long silence that felt like eternity.

"Sorry can you repeat what you just said again please?" Sapphire's voice sounded soft, almost like whisper.

"I said I'm in love with your spirit and I want you to become my woman."

Sapphire looked completely taken aback. It wasn't that she was against what he was saying but more in shock because of it.

"You know," she said finally. "I prayed to the lord for someone and I asked for a sign. I asked that when my man comes, he should identify himself by saying

I'm in love with your spirit. I never told anyone about it and until now no one has ever said that to me."

"Sapphire," said Fela holding her shoulders and looking into her eyes. "Sapphire, this was meant to be, I was made for you and you were made for me. Our God has confirmed it so now let's set our love free."

At that moment Sapphire never spoke but as Fela looked into her eyes they said it all. He saw the wedding, their first house, the babies—he saw it all and he knew at that moment that he was in love.

Lano can be contacted at ukphilosopha@yahoo.com or www.myspace.com/Lano7